RAINEY ROYAL

DYLAN LANDIS

Published by
Soho Press, Inc.
853 Broadway
New York, NY 10003

Some stories have been published in slightly different form
in the following publications:

"Let Her Come Dancing All Afire" and "Keep My Hands from
Stealing" (as "She Will Be Flesh") appeared in *BOMB*, "Rapture and the
Fiercest Love" appeared in *The Normal School* (reprinted by permission
of *The Normal School*, © 2014 by Dylan Landis), "Trust" appeared in
Tin House and *The O. Henry Prize Stories 2014*, "Baby Girl" appeared in
Black Clock, "Fly or Die" appeared in *Santa Monica Review*.

Library of Congress Cataloging-in-Publication Data

Landis, Dylan
Rainey Royal / Dylan Landis.

ISBN: 978-1-61695-571-7
eISBN: 978-1-61695-453-6
1. Teenage girls—Fiction. 2. Fathers and daughters—Fiction.
3. Musicians—Fiction. 4. Nineteen seventies—Fiction. I. Title.
PS3612.A5482R35 2014
813'.6—dc23

Printed in the United States of America

10 9 8 7 6 5 4 3 2 1

PRAISE FOR *RAINEY ROYAL*

"Dylan Landis's captivating and unnerving novel *Rainey Royal*, set in Manhattan of the 1970s and early '80s, is not a thriller, but it smolders with these loaded questions: How far will an adolescent girl go to gain a sense of belonging; and how can her unaimed sexual power put others, and herself, at risk?"   —Liesl Schillinger, *The New York Times*

"Might make you cringe—whether you were the kind of girl who had a ball thrown at your face during gym or the kind who threw it . . . As Rainey moves into young adulthood, her sexuality becomes so complicated, it's like a second character in the book. There is power there, she learns, but it's the power of electricity with faulty wiring; lights aglow; the house in flames."   —*MORE Magazine*

"It's difficult to remember a novel that was more continually on edge than *Rainey Royal*, a series of fraught moments that never seem to let off any psychic steam . . . so taut, the scenes so emotionally charged, that the breaks in the action are welcome . . . beautifully drawn."
          —*Chicago Tribune*

"Fiery, daring, unforgettable . . . Landis knows bad girls—how their minds work, how they are made, and why they are broken. Best of all, she knows how to make you love them—which you can't help but do as you follow Rainey Royal, the title character, through her 1970s Greenwich Village girlhood. Rainey is dangerous, but her struggles are timeless, and Landis writes about her with prose so elegant and crystalline that as you read, you have to remind yourself to breathe."
          —Natalie Baszile, author of *Queen Sugar*, for the *San Francisco Chronicle*

"Transporting, sensual and musical by turns, appropriately enough for a book about sex and jazz."   —Slate.com

"Landis creates a vivid fictive universe . . . every battle, every transgression is minutely observed . . . line by line, one of the smartest and most exacting prose stylists we have."   —The Millions

"[Rainey Royal is] always pushing the moment further, even when part of her feels like backing down, and the result is a story that feels dangerous—as though something might break at any moment."   —The Daily Beast

"'Hard to handle, Rainey thinks. That's what they say when they talk about me.' The book isn't hard to handle—it's a fast read that consumes the reader from beginning to end—but Rainey's experiences are. Landis takes the time to turn Rainey inside out, revealing the dark underbelly of female adolescence."　　　　　　　　　　　　　　　　　　—The Rumpus

"[Rainey, Leah, and Tina] psychologically torment one another but remain inseparable, and exude cool that masks their vulnerability. Landis depicts a 1970s New York City that is a permissive playground and menacing nightmare."　　　　　　　　　　　　　　　　—Electric Literature

"Tremendous . . . Landis offers a bold alternative of which I hope we see more and more: the novel as feat of compression . . . Crisp, beautiful, often hilarious."　　　　　　　　　　　　　　　　　　　　　—*PANK*

"Stark and fascinating . . . unforgettable . . . The hundreds of little trag-edies painted across the page will leave readers deeply affected as Landis perfectly captures a time period of mad exploration during which lines blurred for young people trying to find themselves." —Shelf Awareness

"Blew me away . . . An amazing character."
　　　　　　　　　　　　　—Daniel Chacón, *Words on a Wire*, KTEP

"[*Rainey Royal*] deals in short, sharp shocks . . . [with] a language of the imaginative and beating heart . . . [Landis] weaves spells."
　　　　　　　　　　　　　　　　　　　　　　—*Bookworm*, KCRW

"*Rainey Royal* is a story about loss and recovery by any means necessary . . . It is a brave book, a provocative book, a book that invites re-reading and discussions as intense as the world it portrays." —Necessary Fiction

"*Rainey Royal* is a tough novel with a tender heart . . . Dylan Landis is an author to be watched."　　　　　　　　—New York Journal of Books

"Brilliant, delicate writing . . . A solid choice for literary fiction readers; it also will be appreciated by those who are interested in narratives that depict the bohemian lifestyle."　　　　　　　　　　—*Library Journal*

"A mesmerizing portrait of a teenager in 1970s Greenwich Village. Rainey Royal's life is wantonly glamorous, degenerate, sophisticated . . . [Landis] has created a kind of scandalous beauty in her tale of the simultaneously fierce and vulnerable Rainey."　　　　　　　　　—*Kirkus Reviews*

In loving memory of my father, Bern Landis
In memory of Jan Gottlieb Moskowitz
And for Dean

CONTENTS

LET HER COME DANCING ALL AFIRE

The patron saint against temptation sits straight-backed in an Italian convent as if mortised into her chair, and she is dead, dead, dead. Her name is Saint Catherine of Bologna, and nuns have been lighting candles at her feet since Columbus asked Isabella for those ships.

Rainey Royal, in the reading room of the New York Public Library, peers at the photo in the book so closely she can smell the paper. Her shiny hair spills over the page. Saint Catherine is not just about temptation: she's the patroness of artists, for Chrissake—just what Rainey needs. She thinks they could be sisters, five hundred years apart. Rainey is an artist, and she *embodies* temptation.

Wisps of smoke from centuries of candles, she reads, have stained Saint Catherine's hands and face mahogany. In the photo, the saint wears a gargantuan habit, her nut-colored fingers laced in her lap. Rainey wears a halter top and holds a dry clay egg in one hand and a silver teaspoon in the other.

While she reads, she burnishes the egg with the back of the spoon on her lap.

In her mind, Rainey lifts the musty black fabric. She looks up Saint Catherine's legs. She sees this: not an old lady's crinkles but the lucent flesh of a fourteen-year-old virgin. One morning, Cath walked out on her rich foster family, with its tutors and grooms, and offered herself to the nuns.

In the cloister, Cath will never listen at night for the marquis padding toward her through chilled marble halls.

Why Cath endured that setup at all is because her own father sent her there, to serve the marquis's daughter. There's always a man, right? So there's always a problem in the house.

It is October 1972, and the problem in Rainey's house is Gordy, who tucks her in. Gordy is the best friend of her father, Howard. She remembers this: hugging her knees on the stairs one night, listening to the grown-ups in the Greenwich Village townhouse where she was born and where Gordy has lived forever. Her mother, Linda, came and went from both bedrooms without embarrassment, so Rainey grew up thinking all married ladies had sleepovers. Downstairs that evening her father said, "Gordy and I share everything." Then a pause, and Howard's voice again, lower, a tone she understood even before kindergarten: "Except for the Steinway, my friend, everything," and then rising laughter.

No one wrote anything about Cath's mother in the book.

No one talks about Linda Royal either, even when Rainey asks.

In the library, she reads how Cath and the marquis's daughter grew up studying at the same table. When Cath walked behind her mistress in the gardens, their silk gowns swished like running water. That's because Cath was given the daughter's lavish hand-me-downs with barely yellowed armpits. Rainey can see it.

Plus Cath got unlimited paper and inks, being good at painting animals and the faces of saints.

"I found her," said Rainey, causing all the library people at the long table to look up. With precise little bursts, she rips out the page on Saint Cath. The woman across from her, tracing a map onto onionskin, yelps.

"Oh, relax," says Rainey. She packs up her egg and her spoon and the folded page and strides down the staircase and out into an autumn rain.

RAINEY IS FOURTEEN, JUST a girl trying to get from the entry hall of the townhouse to her pink room on the third floor when her father, Howard, thumps the sofa in that *sit down, baby* way.

She stops, rain-soaked, in the foyer. The place is too quiet. Not an acolyte in sight. Did he send them upstairs to their own rooms or out for pizza? Usually the first floor is packed with young musicians. Some are students, some strays, but Howard Royal only brings home the best. Three days ago he found two brilliant cellist chicks—*found*, thinks Rainey, like shining orphans. The girls have been ensconced in his bedroom. Like he's really going to jam with cellos. Half the acolytes are guys, who supply part-time money and part-time girlfriends and revere Howard in an appropriately oblique manner. When someone new shows up, they say things like, "What's your ax, baby?" But half are girls who play celestial music and give celestial blowjobs and can't believe they get to jam and party and live in the extra bedrooms of, oh my God, *Howard Royal*.

Rainey hasn't heard the place this silent in centuries.

Howard's at one end of the parlor sofa, clamping a beer between socked feet and a clarinet between his knees. He's adjusting the reed. "C'mere, baby," he says. "Isn't it amazing? We're alone."

On West Tenth Street, *alone* means three people: Rainey, her father, and Gordy, who lounges on the far sofa arm refractive as a patch of snow, from his long, milk-colored hair to his alabaster hands. His jeans are white, too, and he parks a damp white Ked on the upholstery. Gordy Vine is not and never has been an acolyte. He is a horn player and the best musical technician in the house—even Howard says it. But Howard has the charisma. Gordy claims to be albino, but his eyes are green. He pretends to be unaware of Rainey by keeping his head down. He pretends he is not getting sidewalk crud on the brocade. He pretends to edit penciled notes in a spiral-bound score.

He turned thirty-nine last month.

Rainey shifts in the foyer. "What?"

She has a stolen saint in her backpack. Her egg is stolen, too; it is supposed to live on the Studio Art windowsill at school. She holds out her arms to show the damage she will do the upholstery. "I'm soaking wet."

She regrets this instantly. Gordy's attention, like a draft from a threshold, wafts toward her. He doesn't even have to raise his head. Howard blows on the clarinet's mouthpiece, looks puzzled, and says, "Sounds like fish frying." Not much about her father's jazz makes sense to Rainey.

"Get your shoe off Lala's sofa," she says. Lala is Howard's mother. She owns the house, but she lives in an old folks' home uptown. Some days Rainey can talk to Gordy any way she wants.

Gordy smiles. The Ked remains. "Rainey," he says softly. Even his voice sounds albino. Rainey thinks of white plaster walls, licked by the painter's brush.

"I sent the acolytes out to collect sounds," says Howard, as if sounds were lost quarters that winked from gutters. "Sit, Daughter."

She drops her pack, collaborates noisily with a folding chair in the parlor, and sits on it backward while Howard watches with pleased amusement. She smells his body oil: sandalwood.

"That school psychologist called again today," he says, "but I think she's on the wrong track. What do you think?"

Rainey flinches and looks to the ceiling cherubs for strength. The ceiling cherubs are three plaster angels who cavort around a trio of bare bulbs. Their ax used to be the chandelier, but last month Sotheby's Parke-Bernet took it away. The house is shedding its sweetest parts like lost earrings; in return, electricity keeps humming, pizzas keep arriving, and Rainey keeps going to Urban Day.

"Are we getting a new chandelier?"

"Do you know *why* the school psychologist called again?"

"No." Rainey stares off into the kitchen, willing the refrigerator to disgorge a glass of milk.

"I think you do."

"She's full of shit. Can I go now?"

"Look at me, Daughter." He smiles as if indulging her. "It's important to be candid about these things."

Gordy's not-looking at her is now so intense he might as well shine flashlights in her eyes.

Howard, and the smile, persist. "So tell us why the school psychologist is talking about you *engaging* with the male teachers."

The school psychologist always peels and eats an orange while she and Rainey talk. The scent comes back to Rainey in a rush. It is the scent of denial, the innocence that slides over her when Florence, the psychologist, asks how she feels about her mother, her father, the torments she dreams up for that Levinson girl.

Extricating herself gracefully from a straddled folding chair could be problematic.

"Screw you." She knocks over the metal chair as she stands and elbows one of the new cellos, so she barely has to hear her father say under the clatter, *Oh, you can do better than your old dad.*

SOMETIMES RAINEY HAS TO share her room—a ginger operation, a kind of Howard trick.

It is one year after the onset of the blue and white pills. They are prescription, but Howard Royal gets them from a doctor friend and dispenses them daily from packs of twenty-eight. Rainey doesn't need them, but he doesn't believe her. Three weeks white, one week blue—he gives her one every morning with a glass of milk and waits until she swallows. He says things like "That's my girl" and "Because, sweetheart, with maturity comes responsibility."

And it is a year after the summer of Jean-Luc Ponty, when her father had Gordy take her one night to hear Ponty play in Central Park, and Gordy steered her under some trees. She was still thirteen. "You radiate power and light," Gordy told her on the grass. But he is always saying shit like that. It was the only time he lost control, and they still didn't go all the way.

It is 4:00 P.M. on a Friday, and Rainey takes a savage bite of Gordy's grilled cheese. He has been making grilled cheese the way she likes it—and rice pudding and chocolate egg creams—for as long as she remembers.

Howard smiles her up and down. "Sweetheart, your room—"

"Tina is sleeping over Friday and Saturday in *my room*."

Tina is Rainey's best friend. They smoke pot on the roof and take turns reading Howard's pornography aloud to each other. Rainey is positive her mother, whose cool elegance she remembers as seeming somehow beyond sex, never read these books.

"Then Sunday," says Howard. "My brilliant young cellists are in need of your floor. Just for a few days. Open your heart."

She has seen the new cellists, always together—giggling on the stairs or leaving Howard's room. They could be sisters, their faces like two porcelain cups, but one girl is shaped like a cello and one more like a bow.

"My heart?" says Rainey. "My heart is a cell in which candles burn at the feet of Saint Catherine of Bologna." Language is the only turf on which she can stand with her father and joust. Occasionally it works.

"Well, then I pity you," says Howard.

"When the fuck do I get my privacy back?" says Rainey. "Where am I supposed to do my homework?"

What she really wants to know is, where is the place beneath a girl's armpit that the back ends and the *side* begins? She can share her pink room with strangers, but tell her this: Is there a region between back and breast that can, in a proper back rub, be considered neutral?

"Be creative," says Howard.

What if it doesn't *feel* neutral?

"Be creative and be adaptable."

Gordy says nothing. His language with Rainey is often nonverbal. For example, the way he has been tucking her in the past couple of years: sitting on the edge of her bed without moving and sometimes stroking her long hair, as if he were the father and she were the little girl. The hair stroking makes her feel so porous and ashamed that she pretends to be asleep. She has no idea if Howard knows; he sleeps on the second floor, and Gordy and Rainey share the third. What would Howard even say? *He strokes your hair—and?* She wonders if Linda knew before she left last year. Gordy never says it is a secret, yet she senses that her silence is required. She has not told anyone but Tina. Often she wishes she had not.

Rainey would like to ask Tina a few things when she comes over, though she won't. For example: Do Tina's body parts meet clearly at dotted lines, like pink and green states on a gas-station map? Where does she get her God-given ability to not give a fuck?

AND WHAT CAN RAINEY draw from Cath's first miracle, performed after death and underground? The nun's corpse exuded a scent so sweet and strong it rose through the soil and drew all of Bologna to her grave. Rainey can see it: every morning, men and women gather at the mound of earth, inhale deeply, and drop to their knees. All day the perfume clings to them. The grave smells like tea-rose oil!

No, the priest says, what you smell is Easter lily, the flower of Christ—but he is wrong. It's tea rose, the scent of power and coiled-up sex, an oily perfume in a little brown bottle. It's the perfume mothers leave behind when they split, that daughters rub between their toes to someday drive men wild. And after eighteen days, according to the book, the mourners get kind of manic. They love and desire their dead, sweet-smelling virgins even more than they hate and desire whores. They have to *see*. So they dig her up. The women and girls dig very carefully, scraping with silver spoons.

LATE OCTOBER SUNLIGHT SLANTS through shuddering leaves, angling low into the windows. Rainey does her homework sprawled on her pink carpet—when she does it. More often she goes to the museum after school, pulling out a sketchpad, dropping her army pack with its straps and buckles noisily on the floor.

People look up. People always look up. She radiates power and light.

"Have you seen her notebooks?" Howard demands when he is summoned to the school. Rainey looks at him gratefully. They sit across a conference table from two teachers and the principal. It's a cool school. Everyone wears jeans except the janitor. Even the principal wears jeans. Howard calls him Dave. When he calls the science teacher Honor he gives her a long, private smile, as if a waiter were even now carrying in a silver tray set for two. "Her real notebooks, Dave, the ones she draws in. Do you people not know an artist when you see one?"

He pulls a pack of Kools from his shirt pocket, flashing a large watch that Rainey loves, smacks the pack on his hand, and flicks a cigarette toward her. Shocked, obedient, she pulls it out. Next to the cigarette, tucked farther down in the pack, she sees a joint.

"For one thing," says Honor Brennan, and looks sharply at Rainey's unlit cigarette. There seem to be so many things, Rainey thinks.

Rainey does not smoke menthol, and students can't smoke inside the school, and she knows Howard knows this. He lights his own cigarette. She waves the lighter away.

"Come on," says Howard, holding the flame. "Don't be afraid. Regulations are just words on paper." Dave looks at the smoke and coughs. He is wearing a tie-dye T-shirt. It is not impressing anyone, thinks Rainey.

She glances at her teachers, hesitates. "My thumb is burning," says Howard. She can hear what he doesn't say, too. *Fuck 'em if they can't take a joke.* She leans into the lighter and inhales.

"This is highly unorthodox," says Dave.

"Even artists go to college," says the English teacher, Zach Moreno, softly.

"By definition, the artist lives *outside of society*," says Howard, "and mirrors it to itself, whether he goes to college or not. I'm an adjunct, personally, and this is what I teach. Are you noticing any lack of intelligence in my daughter? You're not? Then—ladies, gentlemen—are we really here to discuss a few missed pages of homework for a girl who spends every afternoon in a museum?"

"She could go to art school," says Dave. "There's RISD. There's Cooper Union if she can get in. But she needs the grades."

"What are you grading?" Howard blows a stream of smoke past Dave's head. "I think you should ask yourselves this," he says. "Why does your art teacher ask a girl who can't stay out of the Met to rub an egg with a spoon?"

FRIDAY NIGHT RAINEY AND Tina decide to get high. No occasion—just that Howard and Gordy are playing the Vanguard, with most of the acolytes in tow; just that two months into school Rainey is bored sick. The government is based on a tripartite system, and she's supposed to care about this why, exactly? She's in love with Studio Art; it's got Rapidograph pens, and Rainey can draw anything—Ophelia drowning, Icarus falling, Janis Joplin lusciously dead from smack, with that fabulous throat—but Mr. Knecht assigned some weird shit. They had to form eggs out of raw clay, let them dry for two weeks, and then polish them in an endless, circular motion with the backs of teaspoons.

School did not provide the teaspoons. Rainey took one of Lala's spoons, an English antique sterling spoon that shows a leaping hart. She knows the difference between a leaping hart, which she draws surrounded by William Morris–like leaves, and a leaping heart, which she draws interpretively. Sometimes she draws it so interpretively she has to tear the picture out of her notebook and rip it into little strips and throw them out in different trash cans on her way to school.

The egg polishing goes on for two more weeks, consuming entire art periods. Rainey steals her egg from the windowsill and burnishes during French, world religions, and math.

"What's the fucking point?" says Tina. They are baking their dinner: zucchini muffins. They can't decide if it's better to distribute the whole nickel bag through the batter or roll a couple of joints first.

"My egg is perfect," says Rainey. "It looks like pewter."

Aqua threads trail from Lala's ancient copy of *The Joy of Cooking* as if it has a secret underwater life. Rainey checks the recipe, then pours a dollop of vanilla into the bowl without measuring.

"Now, see, if he told me to rub an egg on a spoon," says Tina, in that husky voice Raincy never tires of, "I'd stick the spoon down his throat."

Rainey readies herself. She always has to mention the one thing that hurts; it's like nudging a loose tooth. "Your grandmother said you could sleep here both nights, right?"

Tina winces. It's a faint movement around the eyes. "Probably." The grandmother is a sensitive subject. Tina turns her back and reaches for a bag of sugar. Her top rides up, revealing an indented waist that Rainey appreciates because it is necessary that they both be sexy, but revealing, also, a little sash of fat, which Rainey relishes because it is necessary that only one of them have a flawless body.

It is after the time Howard said to her, "Next to Tina, you're a centerfold—is that why you hang out with her?" and Rainey, thrilled and mortified, choked out that Tina was her *best friend*, and Howard looked past her at silent Gordy and said, "'The lady doth protest too much, methinks.'"

Tina licks a finger and dips it in the bag of sugar. "You think Gordy might come in our room?"

Rainey brains an egg on the edge of the bowl. She thinks about a redheaded oboist she likes to look at across the parlor till he blushes. She demanded his name once, and he stammered it: Flynn. Howard likes to say he has the only jazz oboist in New York. Rainey is not allowed to bother the acolytes, but she can stare.

Gordy has never come in on sleepovers before—she assumes because she stays up and talks.

"He just checks on me," she says in a low voice. "He never *does* anything."

When Tina laughs it sounds like *huh*. Rainey suddenly feels grateful to have confessed the hair stroking, grateful that Tina doesn't judge. Maybe Tina intuits the back rubs, which only just started. Tina, caught beneath an overhead light that brings out the cinnamon in her hair, has her moments of beauty and perfect understanding.

"If he comes in," says Tina, "can we be mean to him?"

"He lives here," says Rainey, who only knows certain ways of being mean to Gordy.

"You know the kind of mean I mean." Tina orbits her upper teeth with her tongue as if checking the jewels on a bracelet. They have both perfected the Pearl Drops move.

The words *drawing off* come faintly to mind—a lightning rod drawing off the fatal bolt; a sister drawing off a bully. A saint, intervening. Is it cool if the person *drawing off* does not know what she is getting into?

"Stick a knife in his heart for all I care."

"Whoa," says Tina. "Fond of the motherfucker, are we?"

THE FIRST TIME TINA came over, they sat on the carpet of Rainey's pink room, which Rainey thinks of as girlfriend pink, a pink chosen by one of Howard's ex-lovers to coax Rainey out of a black phase. Kids and acolytes are forever telling Rainey what this pink is like: it is Barbie, it is Pepto-Bismol, it is Bazooka bubble gum. But the first time Tina saw it she said, *Oh my God you live in a vagina*, and Rainey said, *Fuck you, Tina*, and the wary warmth of equals was sealed between them.

It is 4:30 in the morning, half an hour after the Vanguard padlocks up. The door to the townhouse opens; Rainey hears young musicians laughing and stairs beginning to creak. She and Tina fake sleep. They have eaten three zucchini muffins each. *Come to the dance singing of love*—Rainey has memorized the entire verse, but she is sure Saint Cath wrote it with a special, spiritual dance in mind, not the kind where you go under the bleachers with a boy. She breathes as slowly as her lungs will let her. She attempts to seal her skin, starting at the toes and working up. Her flannel nightie is as modest as Cath's habit. After several minutes she sees, through her eyelashes, a doorway of light slice across Tina's sleeping bag. She watches Gordy step with agility and night vision into the room and around the bag. He moves the edge of Rainey's quilt, which she sewed herself, and sits, and his weight causes Rainey to tip toward him so their hips touch.

He strokes her hair.

I'm moldering, she thinks. I'm not actually *doing* anything and I'm moldering. But between her toes she smells of tea-rose oil, and she knows she is responsible for sending scent molecules swimming through some primal part of his brain.

"Eew," says Tina. "What are you doing?"

"Checking on Rainey," says Gordy. He rises, though. "Doesn't someone check on you?" No, thinks Rainey, can't you tell? No one ever checks on Tina. Somebody feeds her and keeps her clothed, but she is an untended soul. Gordy stands so close she can smell club smoke on his jeans; she can smell jazz. "What are *you* doing?" says Gordy. He sounds genuinely interested.

"Watching you," says Tina.

Gordy doesn't speak. Rainey doesn't move. She wonders if Tina is *drawing off* now. It feels dangerous. You better stop, she wants to say, but she is faking sleep.

RAINEY LOVES HOW SHE and Tina can sit in certain ways and force certain male teachers to look at them. Sometimes the teachers stammer. Sometimes the armpits of their shirts get dark.

She and Tina have a code for it. They call it The Private Game.

TINA SAYS: "WHAT DO you like, Gordy?"

"I am an honorable man," says Gordy. But he does not leave.

Rainey imagines herself fragmenting into the Gustav Klimt lady, the one made of glinting squares of color and gold.

"You like giving back massages?" Tina says.

Rainey is sure she never said a word about Gordy touching her back. He doesn't do it every time.

It is five hundred years after Cath wrote her poem: *Come to the dance singing of love, let her come dancing all afire. Desiring only him who created her and separated her from the dangerous worldly state.*

As Rainey imagines it, Cath knew all about dangerous worldly states.

"I never go where I'm not invited," says Gordy.

Under the heat of her quilt and the domed, dark canopy,

Rainey conjures Cath at midnight in the marquis's house, faking sleep, waiting for her door to swing slowly open.

"I like back massages." Tina's voice is a cat weaving around an ankle. *You know the kind of mean I mean.* They have never pushed The Private Game this far. Rainey hears the longest unzipping sound in the universe, a sleeping bag, followed by the feathery sound of a T-shirt being pulled up. She opens one eye and sees what Gordy must see: the lunar arc of breast as Tina flips onto her stomach. Not drawing *off*, thinks Rainey. *Drawing in.*

"But if you make one move off my back," says Tina, "it's over."

This is followed by the shifting of Gordy's shape, then silence, rustling. Then silence. Rainey palms the hard, shiny egg under her pillow. She fakes sleep as hard as she can.

Here is Cath's second miracle performed after death: though buried unpreserved, her body never molders. Despite eighteen days in the soil it emerges with the flesh resilient and still scented with tea rose.

Undefiled by men, undefiled by death.

"Excuse me." Tina's voice is a doorbell chime. "That is *not my back.*"

Gordy rocks back on his heels. His voice is calm. "What did I do, Miss T? This is a back rub worthy of a saint."

THEY HAVE CLOCKED MANY hours with Florence, the Urban Day psychologist, lying in their sweetest voices. Tina tells Florence what she tells Rainey and the rest of zip code 10011 and Planet Earth: that her parents pay her to live with her grandmother because her grandmother has immaculate degeneration and is going blind. Rainey tells Florence that she plays jazz flute. She says her mother calls from the ashram twice a week and that her father helps with math and cooks bodacious dinners.

They were sent to Florence for staring inappropriately at the male teachers and doing the Pearl Drops thing. "I don't understand," Rainey said sweetly. "I'm in trouble for paying attention? And I shouldn't cross my legs? That's it?"

"THAT," SAYS TINA, "THAT right there, that's what I'm talking about. Quit it."

The quilt on her bed was Rainey's first. She made it by stitching scraps of Linda's forsaken Jefferson Airplane T-shirt and Indian-print skirts and lacy nighties to a blanket with white satin binding. She cut up wrap dresses Linda wore to her job. No one said she could have the clothes; she took them from the closet. She doesn't use blankets anymore; she's gone to the library. She knows about batting.

Where the quilted bits of Linda intersect, Rainey stitched down left-behind earrings, buttons, torn and lacquered pieces of Kodak photos stolen from Howard's albums. She spent months on her Tailor of Gloucester sewing.

Through her eyelashes she sees Tina burrow into her sleeping bag. "I don't want a back rub anymore," Tina says, and Rainey, in the womb of the quilt, marvels at the expansion of her own night-vocabulary. Quit it. Don't want. Anymore.

"You can stop right now," Tina says, and Rainey repeats to herself, *You can stop.*

"Yes, my lady." Gordy stands, his hair phosphorescent in the hallway light. His hands are still and pale at his sides, like gloves. Rainey wonders what shade of blue his balls are under his jeans and decides on cornflower. Blue balls are the point of the entire exercise, the heart of the Pearl Drops thing, the source of all their power.

"Does it hurt yet?" Tina says.

SUNDAY, WHEN RAINEY COMES home from the museum, Howard summons her to the Steinway with a wave. No one puts anything on Howard's piano: no ashtrays, no sheet music, no beer bottles, no rosin, no Harmon or wolf or Buzz-Wow mutes, no toilet-paper hash pipes, no framed family photos because it's never been that kind of house. Fantastic sound is thumping through the parlor, with a heavy backbeat that Rainey likes. She stares down Flynn, who flushes and studies his fingering. He spends a lot of time waiting his turn. He reminds her of one of those long-legged birds that take delicate steps with backward-hinged knees. When Howard finally stops playing, Gordy lowers his horn, the snare stops clicking, and finally the winter draperies, which have stood through two summers in mournful dark red columns since

Lala's departure, suck up the last of the sound. The room is half empty, not everyone plays every time, and Rainey has no idea if there's a schedule. Far beneath the jazz she hears the rattling of the air conditioner, which Howard hates, but he has to keep the windows closed for the neighbors and stop by nine at night.

Some of the acolytes stare at her with fascinated and hungry eyes, for she has constant access to Howard Royal, and she is as untouchable to them as a veiled novice.

Rainey opens her arms and rotates slowly. "'Come to the dance singing of love,'" she says, and feels her powers grow. "'Let her come dancing all afire.'" It was in the book, and now it is in the folds of her burning brain. She does not know what she is trying to provoke. She wants to prove she is protected.

Gordy laughs aloud. The laugh says, *You are beautiful when you are nuts.* Her father says, warningly, "Rainey." She turns on him a gaze like a shield. Who knew she had a shield in her head and a saint in her pack?

"I hope you cleared your perpetually messy floor. I promised the cellists you'd share. A few days, Daughter." The electric violinist, Gemma, shivers visibly as if the room has chilled. Everyone knows the cellists could double up with other acolytes. "Be generous," says Howard softly. He would resemble Christ, Rainey thinks, if his beard did not receive the trimmer and the comb—a weekly father-daughter ritual he taught her young and that she could live without.

"So," she says tightly, "I'll just go up and move my shit."

Rainey turns away as the flautist, Radmila, plays a patter of high notes. It's water, dropping leaf to leaf through the rain-forest canopy: Rainey can see it. *Don't try to understand jazz,* Gordy said once: *You are jazz.* A few times he has whispered, *You're awake, aren't you?* She keeps faking sleep, as if she has left West Tenth and gone far away. Is she saving herself or is she moldering?

Howard's musicians start touching their instruments again. Rainey, stranded, takes the stairs alone to her pink shell of a room.

It's too late.

The cello-shaped chick and her friend, kneeling at the bureau, are dropping her clothes piece by piece into two piles on the rug. Keepers, she realizes, and rejects. "The fuck you are," says Rainey, and slams her fist into the open door.

They raise their porcelain faces. "We're just borrowing." The friend holds up a T-shirt that Rainey doctored with grommets and lace inserts. "This is gorgeous. He said we could share the room, so we figured . . ." Behind her, two cellos bask on the bed.

Rainey stalks in and grabs a cello by the throat. "You want to put that shit back?"

When she and Tina talk like this in the girls' room at school they can make anyone do anything. But these girls are older. They gaze at her, waiting to see what she has in mind for the hostage cello. Rainey jerks it hard. The instruments knock together and hum, and the girls clamber to their feet.

"Clothes and whatever else you stole," says Rainey. "Are those my earrings?"

Miss Cello works at her earlobes. "Please, may I have my cello?"

"Oh, are we at *please* now?" says Rainey, buoyed. "If I let it go, will you leave the house?"

Miss Cello tugs a key from her pocket and turns it triumphantly in the air. "Howard Royal gave me this."

"Cello," Rainey reminds her.

Miss Cello only pretends to know joy on this earth: Rainey can feel it. Miss Cello keeps her gaze on the ground, on filthy stars of chewing-gum foil and bottle-cap planets. Whereas Cath, dead and in the soil for eighteen days, looked at the earth particles all around her and was awed by every turning molecule.

Rainey drags the cello off the Linda-quilt. It makes a scratching sound across the buttons and thumps to the rug. The first girl lunges for it, and Rainey draws back her foot and says, "I'll kick it. I really don't care." She's only wearing Converse, but the girls freeze in the frosted cupcake that is Rainey's room. "You can have it in the morning," she says, "if you don't steal anything else." Of course, they have already stolen everything.

She drags her prize into Gordy's room, pulls it inside, closes the door, and considers. Then she looks back out in the hall. Miss Cello is darting down the stairs, and her friend leans out from the doorway of the pink room.

"You should know that Howard does not give a fuck," says Rainey.

"Seems like Howard doesn't give a fuck about his daughter, either," says the friend.

Rainey picks up a yellow ceramic ashtray from Gordy's bureau and hurls it. The girl ducks and laughs. The ashtray hits the doorframe and falls without breaking. Miss Cello bolts back upstairs. "That bitch," she says, and spots Rainey. Her eyes fill.

"I can't go to school without my cello," she says. "Why are you doing this?" If she got centered in that body of hers, she could be a totally different chick. Move like *this*, Rainey wants to tell her, and you could have men aching to draw a bow across your hips. But Miss Cello doesn't want power. She wants to feel safe. Rainey sees through the eyes of Cath that she will never be an artist.

"Howard says give it back or get out." The girl rubs her hands together frantically.

Rainey gazes at her till Miss Cello's face contorts through several changes of expression. Give it back, or get out—this has to be a lie; Howard has no time for the settling of squabbles. Her mother got out; she sloughed off West Tenth Street to find God on the ashram in Boulder, Colorado. Lala descended the stairs weeping, in the arms of two ambulance men. But Rainey will hold fast to her pink room the way Boston ivy grips the sills outside the garden windows.

Heavy footsteps begin an ascent. Gordy's white-blond

head bobs into view. "Raineleh," says Gordy. He picks up his ashtray, sits on the top step, and stares at her through the spindles, ignoring the cellists. "Are you being a little troublemaker?"

"No." Rainey wheels around and locks herself in Gordy's bedroom with the cello. "I'm fucking things up majorly," she yells through the door.

Sometimes she comes to the dance singing of love, and sometimes she is deep in the dangerous worldly state. She is not sure which would be accurate now. When Tina asked Gordy, *What do you like?* it seemed like a good question. Rainey likes rubbing silver against clay until clay turns to pewter: alchemy.

Gordy's room smells like socks. Outside his windows, a tree flips its leaves to their metallic backs. On the floor, the cello lies naked and bright.

Rainey drags it onto the unmade bed. She takes off the diamond ring her mother gave her, the one that belonged to Linda's mother. She settles herself and with the diamond begins scratching an image into the instrument's back. In the hall, people knock and test the doorknob. Safe in the room, Rainey is making art. Through the windows, the sky bruises. Around her, honey-colored dust sifts onto the unwashed sheets.

Five minutes pass, an hour, she has no idea. Voices rise, and she ignores them.

When the door flies open, it slams the corner of Gordy's bureau so that everything on top jitters. Howard, large in the doorway, does not look so Christ-like now. "If you don't release that goddamn cello, Daughter," he says, "you can get thee to a nunnery for all I care."

Rainey slips her ring back on, grabs Gordy's penknife off his night table, and stands on the bed. The cello stands with her. It is her spruce-and-maple mother. It is her saint against temptation, though she can't resist testing her hold on the pink room.

Watching Howard, she opens the penknife, slides it against the fingerboard, and slits the thickest string. It snaps with a wiry groan. What was the other thing Tina asked that night? Her father crosses the threshold with an angry stride. She is scared, but his anger feels better than when he smiles her up and down. She steps behind the cello but looks him in the eye.

"Does it hurt yet?" she says.

RAPTURE AND THE FIERCEST LOVE

On Monday Rainey witnesses the sorrow of Miss Honor Brennan, who wears a crucifix tucked under her clothes. Miss Brennan suggests they eat lunch together after class, at her desk. Revoltingly intimate, to see a teacher's lunch, its homemade sandwich and nicked pear.

"I didn't bring lunch." Rainey holds her pack to her chest and backs away.

Miss Brennan dangles a rumpled brown bag and says, "I'll share." She has a widow's peak that sculpts her glowing, blue-eyed face into a heart. "I think you could use a chat."

"I'm fine." Rainey's hand is on the doorknob. The only thing keeping her in the science lab is curiosity.

"Yes, I agree you're doing a tremendous job of holding it together," says Miss Brennan. "But people are saying things." She touches her crucifix through the starched fabric of her blouse. Sometimes it works loose. Rainey has seen it. "I can't believe they're all true, but I'm asking you to stay and talk." She is the prettiest teacher at school; she has to be dating one of the male teachers, right?

"Oh, for Chrissake," says Rainey, but she doesn't exactly fling herself out; she wants to hear what people are saying.

"Please," says Miss Brennan, "sit, and tell me about your mother, Rainey. I understand she left."

Rainey slowly closes the door. "She didn't *leave*. My mother took a year to study Ashtanga Vinyasa yoga at an ashram in Boulder, Colorado." She went to the library for this one. She goes to the library for everything. Miss Brennan looks at her steadily. "When she comes back she'll be certified to teach it," says Rainey. "We talk twice a week."

Miss Brennan sucks in her lower lip and nods. "Sit down, Rainey."

Rainey stays at the door.

"Your father says she never calls. He didn't make a secret of it at our parent-teacher conference. Please. Sit."

"She calls when he's not home." Rainey scuffs over to a chair and drops her pack on it. "*Ob*viously. He doesn't know we talk. We talk about art. She's my *mother*."

Miss Brennan gestures firmly at the chair. "You can always leave," she says. "Have a pear."

Rainey sits tangentially. First she dislodges her pack. Then she shoves another chair out of the way. She does not have a pear.

"The teachers who care about you are wondering," says Miss Brennan in the same soft voice, as if she were slowly wrapping Rainey in cashmere, "if you need help with your home situation. I don't mean to pry, but"—she takes a delicate bite of her sandwich, which has a petticoat of lettuce around the edges—"some teachers have heard it's like a commune. The word *cult* came up. Is it true, Rainey, that your father has a lot of young people living there?"

Rainey looks at her, amazed. Do people think her mother abandoned her to some cult?

"It's none of your business," she says.

"I'm making it my business." Miss Brennan bites deep into her sandwich, and Rainey senses that she cannot, in fact, always leave.

"My father," she says, "runs—it's like a boarding school for brilliant jazz students. I live in a house full of music." She chooses her words carefully. "It's very creative," she says. "My home is a very nurturing place."

Miss Brennan pushes the pear closer to the edge of her desk. "Eat," she says. "Where do these brilliant jazz students sleep?"

With Howard, thinks Rainey. "It's a five-story townhouse," she says. "We have like a zillion bedrooms."

"Is that enough?" says Miss Brennan. "Your father is very . . . charismatic. I've met him. Is there any . . . adult activity going on that might make you uncomfortable? Do you feel safe in that house, Rainey?"

"It's *my house*. I feel two hundred percent safe." Raincy stands, pushing the chair away. It screeches.

"People are concerned for you, Rainey. No one is gossiping. Don't be angry." Miss Brennan stands, too. "One more question. Please. Is it true there's a man living there who isn't related to you?"

Rainey possesses an expression of baffled innocence, and she puts it on now. "Gordy? My cousin?" She waits for doubt to register on Miss Brennan's face. "He's lived there since I was two."

Miss Brennan says, "Your cousin."

"He's a genius on horn," says Rainey. "He and my dad play in the best clubs."

Miss Brennan nods. "Rainey," she says, "if you ever need to chat, I'm here. It can be hard without a mom. I think things are tougher than you let on."

The English teacher, Zach Moreno, always sits with Miss Brennan at lunch. And he is gorgeous, too. Mr. Piriello is fat, and Mr. Noble is craggy in a romantic way, but he is old. So, Mr. Moreno. It is like matching up Barbie and Ken, Rainey thinks. Maybe there is something she can do with that. Maybe she could flirt with Mr. Moreno more. In her mind, she picks up her chair and smashes Miss Brennan's head. Only when she can see the blood does she shoulder her pack and say in her sweetest voice, "May I go now?"

· · ·

THE PIETÀ BY JACQUES Bellange is the most delicious in the show at the Met, and Rainey is riveted. In the picture, Mary tips her head back and dips her fingertips into the tiny bowl between her collarbones as if holy water might have collected there. Her face is radiant with pain.

It's Monday afternoon, the afternoon of the humiliation. Rainey lets her pack thud on the museum floor and pulls out her sketchbook.

A tour group sifts around the corner. Rainey feels it rather than sees it swelling behind her. "Ah, we love our art students." The guide has a faint Germanic accent. "But this is the one you should be copying, Miss. It's filled with contradiction. Come join us."

Drop dead, thinks Rainey.

After a moment, he goes on in his tour-guide voice. "Let us explore the tension in this engraving by Claude Mellan."

Rainey balances her sketchbook on one arm. The Mary in the pietà is a real woman, not like those stiff ones from the 1400s. She doesn't try to copy the pietà precisely, with its fine hatch marks. Rather she wants to capture the curve of Mary's neck, the folds in her garment, the muscles in the thigh of the Christ.

Never has she seen such muscles in the thigh of a Christ.

"We see Mary Magdalene with two symbols of the religious contemplative," says the guide, and from his accent Rainey imagines him with skis and Alps. "The cross and the skull," says the guide. "We don't know why Mellan omitted the third symbol, the book. And yet, and yet. Look at her, this reformed prostitute. Her robes have slipped. Her hair is undone. She's a lush young woman, our Magdalene. This is a typical pose for her, during her desert days."

Rainey totally sees it. Spiritual, pretty, a little loose, deep into her thoughts, not a big reader. Hair to her waist.

She refuses to look.

In the Bellange pietà, the Mother Mary sits with her legs apart and the body of Jesus on his knees between them, facing the viewer. This Mary is not embarrassed about any damn thing. She may be pure, but she is still a sensual, fleshy woman, caught up in grief.

The thing Rainey doesn't get, as she sketches, is how the Christ stays upright, kneeling, if he's dead. Every muscle is delineated. His nipples are erect. A fold of Mary's hem flutters up strategically across his hip.

"So I wonder," says the guide, as if musing to himself, "does she know? Is Mary Magdalene so transported by religious fervor she does not realize her bosom is bared? Or are the artists telling us, once a whore, always a whore?"

Rainey hears tittering and turns, furious. The engraving is small, but she can tell right away that the Magdalene, a big-boned, dark-haired sexy chick, is dreaming away. She could almost be Mary's daughter. "Can't you fucking *tell?*" says Rainey loudly, causing a guard to take several decisive steps toward her. "She's like totally transported. Jesus Christ."

•   •   •

TUESDAY, FROM THE FIFTH row, Rainey stares at Miss Brennan as if tenth-grade chemistry might save her life. Her gaze savors the heart-shaped face and locks onto the electric-blue irises. Obviously she's listening, right?

Meanwhile, she inches her arm over to the wall where the Erlenmeyer flasks are lined up. Then she closes her hand around one.

She feels Tina encouraging her, without eye contact, from the front of the room. Miss Brennan separates them. A bunch of teachers separate them, especially in gym. They don't know it strengthens Rainey to feed on Tina's energy from a distance, to know what Tina is thinking without meeting her eyes. Like right now, Tina is thinking, *I dare you to eat the egg afterward. Real slow.*

Rainey pretends she doesn't even know what her hand is doing with the flask because she is so riveted by Miss Brennan's every word. Miss Brennan is gorgeous, even if she is like thirty. She looks like Wonder Woman. So here is what Rainey and Tina want to know: If a woman becomes a chemistry teacher *by choice*, does that mean she is a lesbo or hates sex? And are those two things the same?

Rainey has some unanswered questions in this department, but one thing she knows for sure is how to coax the fat glimmering hard-boiled egg in her lunch bag down the skinny neck of the Erlenmeyer flask.

When she has slid the flask right in front of her, she dips her hand into her pack, finds her lunch, and slips the peeled hard-boiled egg out of its Baggie, never taking her gaze off Honor Brennan.

She balances the egg on the lip of the flask, where it nests, ovoid and shiny, stuck on the neck of the bottle like a fat stopper.

Miss Brennan radars onto her. "Absolutely not," she says. "What lab are *you* doing?" In that moment—Rainey can feel it—Miss Brennan loses Andy Sakellarios, who looks at the egg and laughs hoarsely. She loses Tina, separated by four lab tables but communicating mischief telepathically. She loses Mary Gage, who peers over the collar of her rabbit-fur jacket with wide eyes.

"Egg," says Miss Brennan, pointing at it. "Trash," pointing near her desk. "Immediately." She loses Leah Levinson, who glances only at the base of the flask, and Rainey knows why: she's afraid to look Rainey in the eye.

Hard to handle, Rainey thinks. That's what they say when they talk about me.

She flips her hair over her shoulder, a long, sensuous gesture involving a dramatic arm flourish, because her hair comes down past her waist.

"Miss Brennan?" she says sweetly. "I really, really want to make this egg go down this hole. It'll just take a minute. Please? It's science."

Rainey keeps her voice low and says *hole* as if she were blowing a smoke ring, or a kiss, which makes the boys grin.

"It's third-grade science," says Miss Brennan, "and there

is no food in my class. Throw it out, now, Rainey, I'm not kidding."

Rainey is busy. It's this thing she does with her hair, combing it with her fingers, looking around, catching her friends' eyes and laughing—she has it down. "But I *like* third-grade science," she says in a little-girl voice. She thrusts her shoulders back. If Miss Brennan is having sex with a male teacher, she wants her to think about that teacher trying not to look at Rainey's bust in class. Miss B doesn't have that kind of bust, the kind her own father has special words for. "I have a lighter," Rainey entreats—her way of announcing that she smokes, in case there is still someone who doesn't know—and she tears a thin strip of paper out of her notebook. "Please? Can I? It'll take ten seconds."

She flicks the lighter and waits. The flame wavers near her thumb. The class is mesmerized.

"You are this close to detention. But ten seconds, yes," says Miss Brennan, and Rainey knows she is thinking: *Abandoned girl, confused girl, give her a little rope.*

Rainey is running the class now. "Oooh," she says, "thank you," and squirms on her stool. She takes the egg off the neck of the Erlenmeyer flask. She lights the strip of paper on fire, drops it into the flask, and sets the egg on top again.

It takes only a moment for the air pressure inside to decrease and for the flask to suck in the egg—for the egg to stretch and narrow itself into the neck of the flask. The egg plops down inside with a tiny bounce, lands on the charred paper, and puts out the flame.

"Oh, my God, I love that," cries Rainey. "Thank you, Miss Brennan."

Miss Brennan thrusts her hand out and says, "Flask, Rainey. That happened because the air pressure inside did what? Andy?"

But Andy Sak has his back to her and is looking directly at Rainey. When it's clear he won't turn away, Rainey lifts the flask, joggles it till the egg is in position, and blows into the opening.

Not one eye is on Miss Brennan.

"Rainey, get up here. Bring the flask." Miss Brennan slaps the edge of the desk. "At the board, Rainey, now. I want the formula for pressure versus temperature if a gas is at constant volume. Now."

"I have to get it out," says Rainey helplessly, and holds the flask upended over her palm. The egg narrows again, slithers into the neck of the flask, and drops neatly, warmly, wetly, into her hand.

"Lunch," she sings.

"Five points off your grade," says Miss Brennan. "Throw out the egg out and write the formula."

"It's got p's and t's," says Rainey. "But I forget it exactly. I'm sorry." She looks contrite. Then she takes a slow bite out of the egg. *This is for you, Tina.*

"Ten points off. Throw out the egg," says Miss Brennan.

"I know why you are doing this, Rainey. But just because you have trouble at home doesn't mean you get to inflict it on us."

The silence in the room creaks and shifts. Someone coughs. Rainey stares into the eyes of Miss Brennan as if to drill a hole in her skull.

"It's. My. Lunch," she says softly. She extends the tip of her tongue, which she knows is pretty because she has studied it in the mirror, and licks a bit of ash off the egg. The heads of boys lock almost audibly into position.

Miss Brennan picks up her wastebasket, walks over to Rainey, and slams it on the floor. "Drop it," she says through her teeth.

"I'm hungry." Rainey knows she is going too far, but Miss Brennan went farther, and besides, she no longer knows how to throw out the egg.

Across the aisle Angeline Yost whispers, "Fight, fight." Leah laughs, but when Rainey angles her a look she goes to work on a fingernail with her teeth. Miss Brennan's eyes are bright as glass. "In addition to the ten points," Miss Brennan says, "you have detention."

Rainey mouths a word that is silent but unmistakable and takes another bite of the egg. Leah emits a tiny gasp.

"Detention's Mr. Moreno today, isn't it, Miss Brennan?" says Rainey. "You know his schedule, right?"

She holds the half-eaten egg high above the trash can and waits, watching Miss Brennan's face until color flows into it.

"Thought so," she says. She drops the egg into the trash. It thumps.

Earlier that semester Rainey went to the library, her second-favorite place, and looked up the name. She held the word close till she needed it.

"*Brennan*," she says musically, deciding that today, even as she loses, she wins. "That means 'sorrow' in Irish, right?"

MR. MORENO'S CLASSROOM HAS pictures of the authors around the room. George Eliot, who was a woman. Fitzgerald, whose wife was crazy. There is no keeping up with English lit; you could read and read and never get through it, whereas one day she will have seen every painting in every museum in New York City.

"Can I sketch?" says Rainey from the doorway.

"You can do homework, in silence, Rainey."

She bites her lower lip as if a camera were trained on her, but Mr. Moreno just sits at his desk reading student essays. He has his aviator glasses on, and his hair is as dark and lush as Miss Brennan's. Sometimes they share a Thermos—they *have* to be having sex, Rainey thinks. Their *hair* has to be having sex.

She takes a seat in the front row where she will be maximally distracting and watches his pupils dart back and forth, tracking the handwriting. *Her* handwriting. He makes notes with a red Bic pen.

"Mr. Moreno," she says softly. "I have a problem."

"You do," he says, without looking up. "You're talking."

"That's not it," she whispers. She has no idea what she is going to say next. She is all out of hard-boiled eggs.

"You have a problem with this essay," he says. He looks up and seems to realize, suddenly, that he has a chance to connect with her. "This could be a good time to work on it, actually. You don't fully support your thesis. Here, where you talk about the relationship between wealth and honor—"

Honor Brennan. Dishonor Brennan.

"I don't remember what I wrote," says Rainey, and rises from her chair. "I have to see."

"Stay right there," says Mr. Moreno. His voice is a closed door.

"I just need to see," she says in her little-girl voice. She plants her palms on the front of his desk and leans forward. And then Mr. Moreno says something that doesn't make sense.

"I'm bulletproof, Rainey." He looks directly into her eyes. "Are you?"

At that moment Honor Brennan knocks and steps into the classroom with textbooks in her arms. She looks from Zach Moreno to Rainey's chest and says drily, "Am I interrupting?"

Rainey scuffs back to her seat but turns it sideways. She opens her knees wide, like Mr. Bellange's Mary, and sprawls.

"I thought I'd take over, Zack," Miss Brennan says. "Rainey and I have a few things to iron out."

"Oh, Jesus," says Rainey.

"I'll meet you in the lounge," Mr. Moreno tells Miss Brennan. To Rainey he gives a small, courteous nod.

"Leave me a ciggie, Zach," says Rainey, but he doesn't even smile. When the door closes, Miss Brennan perches on the edge of the desk. Rainey bobs out of the chair and starts pacing. "I need a smoke," she says.

Miss Brennan keeps the textbooks on her lap. *Shield*, thinks Rainey. "Once again I find myself asking you to sit," says Miss Brennan.

"I'm done sitting. I'm done *talking*." At the back of the classroom, Rainey looks out the window over East Eighty-Seventh Street, where kids leave school and stream down the block as if they had all the time in the world. "I need a cigarette," she says.

When she turns and sees Miss Brennan, though, she realizes she is wrong. The cigarette is nothing. Miss Brennan, gazing at her and fingering her hidden crucifix, is the one with the need. She needs to fix Rainey Royal.

Rainey stares at the dagger's point of hair on her teacher's forehead, opens and closes her mouth a few times, and says, "Miss Brennan." Then she falters.

She is *so good*.

"Yes, Rainey?"

"I want—" She looks at the floor.

"What is it, Rainey? What's troubling you?"

She hesitates. "It's embarrassing."

Miss Brennan leans forward. "You can tell me anything, Rainey."

In a voice not much above a whisper, Rainey says to the floor, "I just need to be held."

"You—oh, I knew there was something under all that behavior."

Rainey holds her ground and waits.

Miss Brennan puts her books on the desk. She walks all the way down the aisle. She wears black trousers with low heels and a white cotton blouse buttoned to her neck and a gold cross where Rainey can't see it. She clasps Rainey's upper arms, looks at her searchingly for a moment, and then enfolds her.

She smells of perfume, deodorant soap, and a tiny bit of sweat. Rainey likes it. It is the smell of Wonder Woman. Miss Brennan hugs her the way women hug, shoulders touching but with a natural distance between the chests. Rainey counts to five, then slowly begins to melt into the shape of that distance. When she inhales, her breasts press into Miss Brennan's breasts. When she exhales, her breath washes over Miss Brennan's neck and disturbs her thick, dark hair.

Miss Brennan seems to have stopped breathing.

"Oh, my God," says Rainey, her arms around Miss Brennan's waist. She is alive, she is incredibly alive, she is running the class. "Miss Brennan," she whispers, "will you do something for me?"

Miss Brennan begins to disengage from the hug like a cat that has been held too long. "What is it, Rainey," she says.

"Will you kiss me?"

Miss Brennan steps abruptly back, though they are still, in some way, interlocked. Rainey feels herself scrutinized. She turns her face away and bites the side of her thumbnail.

She gives Miss Brennan time to recollect how an abandoned girl would be—troubled, shy, desperate for affection.

Miss Brennan hesitates, then swiftly leans in and kisses Rainey on the cheek.

Rainey touches her fingertips to the side of Miss Brennan's face.

Then she touches her lips to Miss Brennan's mouth.

For one second, two seconds, there is only shock.

Then Rainey could swear Miss Brennan moves her mouth, or perhaps it is just her head, ever so slightly.

And for a second or two after that it's as if their hair is kissing. But already Rainey's brain is working on another problem. She tips her head back, exposing the tiny bowl between her collarbones. She ignores the little cry of disgust, or is it despair, from Miss Brennan, and the firm shove, and she thinks about what is wrong with Jacques Bellange's pietà—what's wrong, in fact, with every pietà in the Met, right?

"I gotta go," she says, and she stalks to the front of the room to grab her pack. She barely notices Miss Brennan wiping her mouth on her sleeve, barely hears her calling, "Rainey. Don't you dare walk out on this." Studio Art II has oil pastel crayons; maybe the door isn't locked. In *her* pietà, the person draped between the Virgin's knees will be Mary Magdalene, very much alive, a loose, dreamy chick who doesn't like to read; and the Virgin Mother's face will be lit not by sorrow but by rapture and the fiercest love.

TRUST

"We're just practicing," says Tina.

"We're just playing," says Rainey.

"We're just taking a walk."

"Yeah, but we're walking behind *them*," says Rainey. She and Tina have turned right about twenty feet behind a couple who lean into each other, slowly strolling, and here is something Rainey has noticed: couples don't attend to their surroundings the way solo walkers do. She wonders if the gun in her purse has a magnetic pull, if it wants to be near people.

"We're losing them," says Tina.

They're playing robber girls. Before they took the gun out for a walk, Rainey and Tina were up in Rainey's room wrapping tie-dye scarves around their heads to disguise their hair. They put on cheap lime-green earrings from Fourteenth

Street to take attention off their features and T-shirts from
Gordy's room, across the hall, to hide their own tops.

The earrings and T-shirts will go in the trash right afterward, that's the idea.

Would go. They're just playing.

The man and the woman amble on through the purpling
evening, past the trees that encroach on the sidewalk.

"Gordy didn't mind you going through his stuff, huh?" Tina's
T-shirt says LARRY CORYELL on the front and THE ELEVENTH
HOUSE on the back. Rainey's says CHICK COREA. Hers is signed.

Rainey regards Tina as they walk. She wonders if the
question is loaded. Tina is the only person on earth who
knows about Gordy's night visits. But they are best friends.
Plus Rainey doesn't want to be one of what her father calls
those eggshell people.

She says, guardedly, "If he figures it out, he'll be pissed.
But he won't. I'm never in his room."

Ahead of them, the couple slows to look up at the window
of a townhouse, and Rainey stalls by bending over to retie
her sneaker lace.

Tina makes a little smirk sound in her nose. "Yeah, why
would you be," she says. "He's in *your* room every night." Her
hand fastens to her mouth. "Oh, no," she says through her fingers. "It just came out. I'm sorry, Rain."

Inside Rainey's purse, the gun beats like a heart. Its work-
ings are a mystery. She and Tina were afraid to check if it
had bullets because of the little lever that looks like another

trigger. Rainey thinks the round part might be called a *chamber*, which sounds romantic.

"It's okay," says Rainey. What else is it her father says? *Fuck 'em if they can't take a joke.*

Through the darkness that drapes them all, she studies the woman who walks ahead of them. She's tucked her sleek hair into her collar, implying some magnificent length—*like mine*, thinks Rainey—and she wears Frye boots, which make a lovely, horsey click on the sidewalk. It's not enough for this chick to hold the man's hand; she has to nestle both of their hands into the pocket of his leather jacket, a gesture that irritates Rainey and makes her think, bizarrely, of the airlessness of that pocket, of lying under her quilt at night, waiting to see if her door will open and faking sleep.

How do you say no to an innocent back rub? She had finally asked Tina that.

"It's not okay," says Tina. "I can read you. It was a shitty joke, Rain. It just came out. I don't know why."

As they walk on, Rainey can see what the man and woman stopped to admire: a red room hung floor to ceiling with paintings. "Really," she says. "It's okay." She smiles sweetly at Tina. It isn't clear who's being punished by the sweetness.

What kills her is the woman's cape. It flaps serenely behind her calves like a manta ray. Sometimes when Rainey meets her aunt Laurette for lunch, Laurette wears a cape, which connects it somehow with her mother.

"Swear it's okay," says Tina.

"I swear." She is still smiling, and it is like smiling at Tina from across a long bridge. Rainey ought to get over it—seriously, fuck her if she can't take a joke.

Tina exhales. "Okay." They both watch the couple for a moment. Then Tina says, "It's not like I need the money."

Rainey opens her mouth and closes it. She's tempted to make a crack, but she holds it in. Tina's been going on about her grandmother a lot—how she gets paid twenty dollars a week to live with her. How the grandmother is blind. Best friends for five years, and Tina has never invited Rainey home, so Rainey's not buying. She's never probed, though. Tina might detonate, or cry.

They've sped up, and now Rainey slows, partly so their footsteps won't be heard, but partly because she is pissed off and wants to consider the ramifications—that she *is* one of those eggshell people and fuck her because she cannot take this particular joke, and she suddenly has had it with the grandmother story, because Tina has never had a twenty in her pocket once. A perverse urge to find the fuse in Tina rises up in her. And it would be so easy. Tina is like one of those sea corals they saw in a bio-class movie that plant themselves any damn where they please but close up tight as a fist when brushed by something they mistrust. In fact the only thing they do trust is this one fish called a clown fish. Rainey isn't anyone's goddamn clown fish.

She says, "I know, Tina. You get twenty dollars a week to live with your grandmother."

Tina looks at her slantwise and reaches deep into the bag on Rainey's shoulder—*for the gun*, Rainey thinks crazily, but it is only for the pack of Marlboros.

"Check out that cape," says Rainey. "That's mine." By now it feels like the cape might have belonged to her mother once, and she is simply reclaiming it.

"What's that supposed to mean, about my grandmother?" Tina lights a cigarette and drops the pack back in the bag.

Rainey wonders if she should be reeling Tina in right now, since they are playing robber girls. Besides, the grandmother is sacred territory. Rainey knows that without being told. Tina is tougher than Rainey, but she is also easier to hurt. Rainey knows *that* without being told. She listens to the slow, steady hoofbeat of the Frye boots, satisfying as a pulse. Can you rob someone of her boots and cape? It's okay to think these things, because they are just playing. They will veer off any minute. The woman looks back, appraises them with a glance, and dismisses them.

"I asked you what it means about my grandmother," says Tina.

"It means your cup runneth over." Rainey uses her musical voice. "If you're getting twenty dollars a week."

"I don't have a cup." Tina's voice is low. "I have a savings account. I'm not supposed to touch it."

"You must be rolling." Now Rainey, too, reaches for the cigarettes, which they jointly own, and lets her knuckles bump the gun. "What bank?" She's ultracasual. The gun is cold and could shoot off her foot, but the weight of it feels good. Already she knows she will stash it at the bottom of her school backpack, with her picture of Saint Cath.

"What *bank*? What is this, a fucking quiz? You don't believe me." Reflexively Tina passes over her cigarette so Rainey can light hers.

"I want that cape, Teen."

The couple turns left on Greenwich, walks a block, and crosses Barrow. Then they turn right on Morton. Rainey and Tina pick up their pace and fall back again, spooling out distance like kite string. It's perfect; they're all headed closer to the Hudson, where only true Villagers live and tourists rarely stray. Even from a half block back, Rainey knows the man is handsome, his hair dark and thick, the shape of his head suggesting broad cheekbones that ride high. Rainey wants this man to desire her even as he looks at the gun and fears her. If she can make him desire her, she'll erase the feeling of Gordy's fingers where they don't belong. Right now the feeling is a dent at the far edge of her left breast. It's a pressure along her neck where he starts stroking her long hair. She wants the cape, and she wants some other things that the man and the woman have. The money doesn't interest her.

"I have over a thousand dollars in Marine Midland Bank," says Tina.

"I'm going to take her cape. You can have all their bread."

"If you don't believe me," says Tina, "I'm not taking another step."

"Oh?" says Rainey in the dangerously charming voice she

saves for the final minutes with a victim in the girls' room. "Do you really live with your grandmother? Or do you just not want me to meet your family?"

Tina stops. Let her, thinks Rainey, she won't stop long. She keeps walking. By the time she makes half of Morton Street by herself, she is trying not to trudge; she is missing Tina acutely, missing the way she bumps into Rainey sometimes, the slight brushing of her jacket sleeve. Tina doesn't go in for hugging, but she finds other ways to make contact, the affectionate shove, the French braiding of each other's hair, touching the hand that holds the match—anything that can't be called lezzie, which suits Rainey fine. When she finally hears Tina approaching at a scuffing trot, she stops and waits, happy and faintly ashamed.

Tina says, "Gimme the goddamn bag, Rain."

Rainey passes it over. She waits to see if Tina is going to detonate and what that will look like. She waits to see if Tina can take a joke.

"I'm sorry, Teen."

Tina looks into the bag as she cradles it in front of her, and Rainey knows she is looking at the darkly radiant gun, a gun Rainey stole from her father's filing cabinet days earlier after one of his obnoxious sex talks. She's spent a lot of secret time in her father's room. She's excavated the postcards her mother sends from the ashram. She's stolen family photos from Howard's albums, one at a time. She's found boxes of Ramses and a pair of leopard-print underwear for men and the dispensers of birth-control pills from which Howard administers one pill to her every morning. *I know what girls your age are doing.* The talks have escalated, and she hates them, Howard loosely strung across a brocade parlor chair while she's curled into her carapace to hide her breasts.

"I believe you," says Rainey. "I do."

In addition to the gun, Rainey stole her birth certificate from a file marked "Legal." *Rainey Ann Royal.* Who the fuck picked Ann, anyway? A girl named Ann would dance badly and her hip-huggers wouldn't hug. If anyone kissed her, she'd wonder where the noses go. In dodgeball, if you were feeling mean, Ann would be the girl whose anxious face you'd aim for.

Maybe Ann is the reason her mother left.

No one knows Rainey's middle name, not even Tina, and she knows every single other thing about Rainey. Tina knows it is a lie when Rainey says she plays jazz flute. She knows it is true that Rainey technically may almost have lost it to her father's best friend. She knows it is a lie that Rainey will move to the ashram to be with her mother when she is sixteen. She knows all this, and she says nothing.

Ahead, near the corner of Washington, the couple sits on a townhouse stoop. They kiss and lean into each other.

"She's blind," says Tina. It takes Rainey a second to realize they are still talking about the grandmother. "I *told* you." They are standing less than half a block from the couple, watching obliquely. The man lights two cigarettes and passes one to the woman. Maybe they are just playing, too, playing at being robbed. The man glances up the sidewalk and watches Rainey and Tina, still in conference.

"I get it," says Rainey. "I believe you. I get it, Teen."

They resume a slow walk toward the townhouse stoop. Rainey could swear she hears Tina thinking hard in her direction. She could swear she hears something like, *I'm lying, she's not blind. The twenty dollars, that's bullshit, too*, and Rainey thinks back, *It's okay, Teen, I love you anyway, and we're going to just walk by these people, right?* and she hears Tina think, *Of course we are, we're just playing*, when Tina drops her hand into the bag and says, "You don't get anything."

They are about a quarter block away. Less.

Alarmed, Rainey looks straight at the beautiful leonine man. "Don't do it," she says in a low voice. And then, because she knows it is too late, because it is not in her control, and because she wants to do it, too, she says quietly, "Don't hurt anyone."

Now the woman looks up. In about fifteen steps, if they keep walking, Rainey and Tina will reach the man and the woman on the stoop.

They keep walking, slowly.

Tina says, "There's a safety, right? That's what it's for, right?" Her elbow is cocked; it's obvious she's about to draw something out of the bag, and now they are right there, steps from the man and the woman sitting and smoking on the stoop, and Rainey has no idea if there's a safety or what a gun was doing in Howard's filing cabinet. She wants the man to look at her and lose all awareness of everything that is not

Rainey, and he is, now, looking at her, but with the wrong expression. Quizzical. He looks quizzical, and the woman is checking his face to see what's changed. Tina stops. Rainey stops behind her. She imagines Tina stepping closer to the stoop and the man twisting her wrist so that the gun falls to the sidewalk and explodes, shooting someone in the ankle. But she wants that softly gliding cape, which she will wear to school, inciting fabulous waves of jealousy.

She could go somewhere around the treetops and look down from there. It's a gift she has, one she likes to think her mother left her. The moment hurtles toward them. She has to decide fast. Tina faces the woman as if she were going to ask her directions. Her two hands shake around the gun, which is abruptly half out of the bag.

"This is a stickup," she says, trembling, her voice hoarse, and Rainey is far from the treetops, she is right there, feeling the concrete through her shoes.

The woman claps a hand over her mouth, stopping a laugh. "Central casting," she whispers from under her hand.

"The gun's real," says the man. "Shut up, Estelle." Rainey has no idea what *wuthering* means, but she thinks he must have that kind of face: brooding and gorgeous, from some dreamy old novel.

"Yeah, shut up, Estelle." Tina sounds like she does in the girls' room but with an undertow of fear. She says, "You guys live here or what?" Rainey feels the approaching moment thundering right up to her. She feels like someone who can take any kind of joke, now. She can't wait to find out what her job will be.

The man and the woman say no and yes at the exact same moment. "Take our wallets," says the man. "You don't have to hurt anyone."

"Be nice," says Tina. "Invite us up."

"If you're going to do anything, do it here," says the man. Estelle's hand remains plastered to her mouth.

Rainey feels ravenous for what is about to happen. The sidewalk is pushing through her shoes now. "I'm feeling kind of antsy down here," she says in a voice that sounds like smoke and jazz. She has it down. "Take us upstairs, baby," she tells the man.

Tina walks up to the stoop and jabs the gun against Estelle's knee. Saint Tina of the Girls' Room—are they really in the same place, doing the same thing? Is it possible that Tina feels purification as she does this bad act? Rainey's father's words unspool from her body as if she is expelling a magician's silk scarf: *They talk about this at school, don't they? How girls your age are growing into their sexual powers?* She feels the nape of her neck sealing itself against Gordy's hand, and she looks at Estelle's neck with rising irritation.

"Okay okay okay okay okay," says Estelle, and gets up fast from the stoop.

"Hey, listen," says Rainey, batting Tina on the arm. She almost says her name but catches herself. "I totally believe you. I do. I had one crazy moment of doubt, but it's over. I'm sorry." She waits while Tina closely scans her face as if she's not sure she's seen it before.

"You still think I'm bullshitting," says Tina, locking her gaze back onto the boyfriend and Estelle. "And you're still mad from what I said about Gordy."

Rainey is not afraid of Tina. She might be afraid of hurting Tina, though.

"I believe you to death," says Rainey. "And it's okay about Gordy. Come on. I'll prove it. Let's do something crazy."

"Oh my God," says Estelle. "Oh God oh God oh God."

THE BRICK BUILDING'S ENTRY hall is lit with bare bulbs, and its stairs are thickly carpeted. Glossy black doors, greenish walls—Rainey feels like she is at the bottom of a fish tank. "Go," says Tina harshly, and the man looks at her jamming her purse, with the gun half in it, into Estelle's back. "Don't touch her," he says, and immediately starts up the stairs. Rainey listens for sounds from other tenants and hears none. "I'm aiming right at Estelle's spine," says Tina, and while it seems to Rainey that the man could lunge back down the stairs at them, it also seems that the word *spine* sounds menacingly like bone porcelain, and she is not afraid.

They climb, first him, then Estelle and Tina in a kind of lockstep, then Rainey, the shag carpeting hushing their progress, till the man stops at a door on the third floor and Estelle sags against it. She says, "You don't have to come in. You could turn around. We'll give you everything."

Tina holds the gun close to her own side, aimed at Estelle. "Oh, we can't wait to see your apartment," she says in a pretend-guest voice.

Rainey holds her hand out for both sets of keys; she senses Estelle and the boyfriend trying not to touch her palm. It makes her powers grow, holding their keys and key chains: such intimate objects. She opens the shiny black door, feels for a switch, and turns on the light.

"You're not *kidding* we want to see it," she says.

The apartment, a large studio with two tall windows, is painted a deep violet, as if an intense twilight has settled. In contrast, the trim and furnishings—a bureau, a table with chairs, and a curvaceous bed frame—are painted bridal white. Rainey can't believe it. She walks down a violet hall into which a Pullman kitchen is notched, flicking on lights as she goes. At the end, she opens the door to a violet bath. She wants to steal all the walls.

Behind her, she hears Tina telling the boyfriend and Estelle to sit on the bed, and how far apart.

"What color is this?" she calls from the bathroom, where the white shower curtain manages to look like a wedding gown against the violet walls.

"I mixed it." Estelle is hyperventilating; she can hear it. "I'm a set designer."

Rainey walks back down the hall and props herself against a white dining chair. Tina moves cautiously around the room, always watching Estelle and the boyfriend, lifting small objects off the bureau and nightstands and amassing a little pile of goods on the hearth. Rolls of coins. Bracelets. The gun never wavers. Rainey asks Estelle, "Yeah, but what do you *call* it, this color?"

"Amethyst," says Estelle. "It's a glaze."

"It's incredible," says Rainey. "It's the most beautiful color I've ever seen."

Estelle hugs herself and shivers. "Please point that somewhere else," she asks Tina. "I swear I won't do anything."

"God, I love this place," says Rainey. "Would you light me a cigarette? And may I have your cape, please?"

RAINEY WATCHES TINA COLLECT sixty-three dollars from the two wallets tossed on the table and a fistful of silver earrings from a bureau drawer. It takes only a minute. Tina never stops watching Estelle and the boyfriend. She jams her prizes into the pocket of the boyfriend's leather jacket, which she is now wearing. Then she positions herself by the white marble hearth. Estelle and the boyfriend are not playing at being robbed. They sit on the edge of the bed about as far apart as they can while still holding hands—the holding hands was Tina's concession.

Glancing at Tina, Rainey catches sight of herself in the mirror over the hearth, luxuriant hair spilling out the back of the tie-dye scarf. "Look at us." She gives Tina a light nudge. "Even with all this shit on, we're still cute. We should take a Polaroid. You got a Polaroid, Estelle?"

Tina keeps the gun aimed straight at Estelle as she turns quickly to look at herself in the mirror, then at Rainey. Her shoulders slump a little. She looks back at Estelle but says, "How can you tell it's still us?"

Rainey laughs. "You're tripping, right?" Tina shrugs. They both know she hasn't tried acid yet. "'Cause it looks like us," says Rainey. "Right?"

"I'm not sure," says Tina.

"You're on blotter," says Rainey, and waits for her to stop being spooky. Rainey once licked blotter off Gordy's palm and spent hours watching the walls quilt themselves exquisitely, kaleidoscopically. "Who else would you think I am." says Rainey. "Jimi Hendrix?"

"I know what Jimi Hendrix looks like. Don't move," Tina snaps at the boyfriend, who is edging closer to Estelle. "I *am* tripping," she says. "I don't recognize myself."

Rainey isn't sure she recognizes this Tina either, the one who sees a stranger in her own face. "Ever?"

"That would be retarded. I mean, with the scarf on."

It's Rainey's turn to *nosy around*, as her father would say. She takes her time. Tina's weirding her out. The nightstand clock says they've been there four minutes. Surely they can stay another four. In the silence she can hear the clock whir. The cape hangs heavy from her shoulders; it is too hot for the apartment, but the weight feels terrific.

On a closet shelf she finds a stack of typed and handwritten letters rubber-banded in red. She takes it down and sets it aside on the bureau. "You don't want that," says Estelle, half rising. "It's old, it's junk—"

"I don't always recognize people on TV, either," says Tina. "Or at school. You think there's something wrong with me?"

"Yes." Rainey goes back to the hallway Pullman kitchen for a pair of shears.

"Well, then fuck you," calls Tina.

"But there's plenty of shit wrong with me, too," says Rainey, walking back in with the scissors.

She snips buttons from Estelle's blouses, lace and beadwork from a vintage sweater, ribbons from a nightgown. She puts these on the bureau with the letters. "In winter?" says Tina. "When you put a hat on? I'm not a hundred percent sure it's you till you say something." She takes a deep breath and locks it up somewhere for a while. "At least I always know my grandmother." She smiles; it's a private, knowing smile. Rainey could almost swear there's pride in it.

She bites her lip. She prowls the room more aggressively. She finds two photo albums at the foot of the hearth and begins robbing them of photographs. "Not my father," says Estelle, and starts to cry. "Not my grandmother."

"Who is this?" Rainey holds up a square color photo of a woman pretending to vamp in a one-piece bathing suit. The woman's smile is playful, as if she is somebody's mother who would never really, actually vamp. Mothers interest Rainey: their presence, their absence, the way they react to the heat waves her body gives off near their husbands and sons.

"No one," says Estelle.

Rainey adds it to the stack. Estelle makes a keening sound

in her throat. Rainey, moving on, seizes two black journals from a nightstand drawer.

"Oh my God, no," says Estelle, but then she looks at Tina and the gun and closes her eyes.

Rainey turns abruptly to face Tina. "Look," she says, "if you ever don't know who someone is, just ask me, okay?"

"Do you think I'm crazy?"

"Just ask me."

"Are we okay?"

Rainey sighs like of course they're okay, but she still hears it. *He gets into your room every night.*

"Do you think I have schizophrenia?"

"Just *ask* me," Rainey says.

She goes down the hall again, cape flapping behind her; she salvages a grocery bag from under the sink, unclips the receiver from the hallway wall phone, and drops that in first. Then she drops in the letters, the cuttings, the photos, and the journals that she has piled on the bureau. The door lock, miraculously, requires a key on each side. She and Tina can actually lock these people in.

"Who's the woman in the photo?" demands Rainey.

Estelle, crying, shakes her head.

"Take my watch," the boyfriend tells Tina. "Leave her papers and take my watch. You'll get fifty dollars for it, I swear."

"Thanks," says Tina, as if startled by his generosity. She makes him give it to Estelle, who holds it out, shrinking from the gun.

"The papers?" he says. Rainey sees Tina admiring the

watch, and she slips into a vision. She sees a tapestry made from scraps of handwriting and snippets of photos, tiny telegrams from the heart: patches of letters, strips of confessions, grainy faces of people who have, in one way or another, perhaps like her mother, split. She'll sew buttons at the intersections, layer in some lace. In Rainey's hands, such things will reassemble themselves into patterns as complex as snowflakes. She will start the tapestry tonight, in her pink room. What would Estelle do with this ephemera anyway, besides keep it closeted away?

"You have Paul's watch," whispers Estelle. "Can I have my papers?"

"Oh, it's Paul?" Rainey looks at the boyfriend. "I don't have Paul's watch." She doesn't, in fact, have a watch at all; she is waiting for her father to give up his. She swirls the cape and turns theatrically to Tina, who appears delicate in the leather jacket. "You have the watch, right?" Rainey sighs dramatically and runs her hands over the cape down the curves of her body, staring at Paul, who looks back at her with the directness of someone who respects the gun too much to move but is not exactly afraid. This intrigues Rainey tremendously.

"I thought Paul would like me better, but *she* got the watch, so apparently not." She's just playing, but it seems to her that Tina looks at her sharply. "Listen," she says to Tina, "let's go. I'm great. I have every single thing I need."

She is surprised to see hurt flash across Tina's eyes.

"You're great?" says Tina. "Why are you great? What've you got that you need?"

Paul sits forward.

"Shut up," says Tina, though he hasn't said anything.

"Don't," says Rainey. She is holding her grocery bag with one arm and has a hand on the doorknob. "I said I believe you. Let's go." But Tina remains plastered to the hearth.

"What've you got that you need?" says Tina. When Rainey doesn't answer, she says, "What? You've got an albino freak who—" She stops, possibly because Rainey is staring her down, possibly out of restraint.

"An albino freak who *what?*" mutters Paul.

Rainey looks at Tina, flaming against the amethyst walls, radiant in her distress. She feels the gaze of Paul upon her. "I have everything I need *from this apartment*," she says, as if talking to someone from a distant land.

"Oh." Tina visibly relaxes, as if warm water were being poured through her. "I don't." She turns a slow, thoughtful quarter circle, looking around the room.

"Oh no," says Estelle. "Please go. Please please please go."

"Get those scissors, would you?" says Tina, taking a step toward Estelle.

Rainey picks them up off the nightstand, where she'd set them down after taking souvenir snippets from Estelle's clothes, and swings them from one finger. "What are you going to do, cut her hair?"

Tina smiles. "No, you are."

"Really? Seriously"—again she almost says Tina's name— "what are you planning to do with her *hair?*"

"Same thing I was going to do without it," says Tina.

Estelle lets go of Paul's hand and clamps both her hands around her hair. "For Christ's sake," says Paul.

Rainey wonders if the gun belongs to Tina now. Estelle's hair belongs to Estelle; that much is true. "No," she says. "This is between me and you."

"You said everything was okay," Tina says. "You said you believed me. You said, 'I'll prove it.'"

"I think she's proven quite a bit," says Paul.

"Whose boyfriend *are* you? Be quiet," says Tina, still pointing the gun at Estelle.

Rainey sets the grocery bag on the floor and puts her face in the bowl of her hands, scissors still dangling, so she can think. Tina is telling the truth now. It's Rainey who's lying: she does not believe a word about the grandmother, and things are not okay. She looks through her fingers from Estelle, who has wrapped her long hair protectively around her fist, to Tina, who waits to see if trust can be restored.

She almost asks again about the woman in the picture. It's the right moment: she holds the scissors, and Tina holds the gun. Instead she takes a deep breath of amethyst air. "Forgive me," she says, and for a moment, while neither Tina nor Estelle knows whose forgiveness she requires, she feels nearly free.

"Here," says Rainey. She bends over quickly, so the tie-dye scarf falls forward and the violet room swings back, grabs a thick sheaf of her own long, dark hair, and cuts.

CLARINET

"Say it," says Rainey. She lounges against a steel countertop, scarred and waxy dissection trays lined up behind her. "*I ride the bus.* Say it."

Lunchtime: the science lab at Urban Day School is deserted. Tina, glowing with menace, blocks the door. We're the lionesses, Rainey thinks.

Leah Levinson is the giraffe. She stands locked by fear behind Miss Brennan's desk. Taxi horns filter through the windows. Rainey stares with arms crossed, daring Leah to look up and escalate things.

The girl appears to be counting floor tiles. She would be so easy to fix, Rainey thinks. Her hair French-braided, some coppery eye shadow to bring out her green eyes. Tighter jeans—Rainey could stitch them. She would teach Leah to dance. She and Tina could make it a project.

Then Rainey could decide if Leah was an acolyte or a friend.

"She doesn't know what the bus is." Tina drops into a plié. Everyone knows what the bus is; it's for crippled kids and poor kids who get into schools in better neighborhoods. At least this is how the insult goes.

"Say *I ride the bus*," says Rainey, "or I'll soak you." She lifts a beaker off a shelf and moves toward the sink. If Leah gets wet she'll panic and change into her gym shirt. Whereas if Rainey had the wet top, she'd laugh with fake mortification at her Sophia Loren bust. That's what her father calls it, her Sophia Loren bust, except he uses a different word.

"All right, now you have to say *I want to give Andy Sak a rim job*." She and Tina exchange a glance. For days they have marveled at this whirring phrase that sounds half mechanical and half obscene. Rim, lid, edges, jars—maybe it has something to do with nipples, Rainey thinks. Or maybe it is a bluff or a misunderstanding.

"Okay, Rain, do it," Tina says.

Rainey sets the beaker in the sink, turns on the tap, and grabs a bottle of formaldehyde. "Guess which." She blocks Leah's view as she pretends to pour.

"I ride the bus." Leah crosses her hands over her chest and watches warily as Rainey approaches with the brimming beaker.

Rainey gives Leah the sweet, sorrowful smile she might give a small child who's resisting bedtime. She feels in herself the power to make Leah trust her, to maybe drink from the beaker. Her father has acolytes—it might be cool to have one of her own.

"I ride the bus," says Leah. "Let me out, okay?"

"Too late," says Tina, "you were supposed to say about the rim job," and Rainey, the word *rim* humming in her brain, approaches the girl sidling along the wall.

THIS IS NEW, AND Rainey hates it: Tina has just two hours after school, and her grandmother believes those hours are for Bible study. Rainey has gone from agnostic to atheist when it comes to believing in the unseen grandmother. Tina's real family must be drunk, mean, or naked. Don't hide it, Rainey wants to tell her—who wants to be best friends with some normal-family chick?

After school they maneuver around the little crowd listening outside the townhouse and enter the foyer, where jazz blares from the parlor. Howard is on the Steinway, his body rocking, hair falling in his face, and Rainey, watching his hands pump, wonders not for the first time if he is pushing music into the massive piano or somehow pulling it out. Gemma, the English acolyte whom Howard found playing in the Times Square subway, whipsaws her bow across the electric violin, which Rainey thinks is the prettiest sound in the world. Her eyelids flutter when she plays. Radmila is on electric flute, and Flynn is there, waiting to play and staring at Rainey. He has a paperback crammed into his back pocket. She has never seen another acolyte with a book.

"Ignore them," says Rainey, because lately Tina has been lingering in the parlor doorway like a climbing vine, dribbling away precious ticks of her already diminished one hundred twenty minutes.

But the brass is glinting, the piano is brilliant, and Tina snags on the doorframe. Rainey doubles back to tug at her and sees Howard wave *cut*.

"The delectable Miss Dial," says Howard, and Rainey watches Tina respond as if she were being tuned. Her shoulders pull back, a hip curves out, and she looks down with a shy smile.

"Come on, Teen."

"Do you like what you hear, Tina?" Howard asks, as if the fates of his young musicians, who wait patient as horses, are in her hands, or as if, perhaps, he is talking about something else entirely.

Tina glances at Rainey. Then, almost imperceptibly, she nods to Howard. Rainey shakes her head and goes back to eye-flirting with Flynn. Howard's daughter may be off-limits to the male acolytes, but she and Flynn have been trying without words to arrange a meeting. Every time Rainey looks up, meaning *roof*, he frowns at the ceiling, perhaps meaning, *Where the chandelier used to be?* or else, *In your bedroom, are you out of your mind?* She is not out of her mind. She is fifteen and on the pill. *A girl your age is a fully opened flower,* her father says.

"It's still in composition," says Howard. "But if you respond to the finished piece, let us name it in your honor. 'The Tina Temptation.' What think you, Gordy?"

"Tell him it sucks, Teen," says Rainey. Howard is stealing everything: her two hours, her best friend, the light he normally shines on her.

Or maybe Tina is the thief.

"It's not about you, Tina," says Rainey. "He might as well call it 'The Howard Ego.'"

Howard laughs deeply. Gemma raises her bow and produces a ribbon of sound, but Howard raises his hand. "One more thing," he says, and Rainey feels his interest sweep across her like a searchlight before it returns to Tina. "How's the clarinet coming?"

Tina inhales sharply.

"Did you forget to tell her, Miss Temptation?"

"How's your *clarinet*?" demands Rainey. *Mistemptation* sounds to her like a yearning gone wrong. "Tina doesn't take clarinet. She doesn't take anything."

"I do," says Tina quietly. "At school. It's coming fine."

"You don't have a clarinet." Rainey swallows; this is not what she means. Howard smiles. All the acolytes are looking at them.

"I showed her the fingering," says Howard. "She might have a nascent talent."

He showed her the fingering—and where was Rainey? Upstairs, thinking Tina had gone home? She can see it, how he stood behind Tina Dial, placed his hands over hers, inhaled her hair, his attention like the light from a star that has wheeled in close. Closer. Oh, Tina. No wonder she didn't tell: she fell.

"Nascent, that's great," says Rainey. "Are you coming or not?"

"Five minutes."

Howard pounds out two notes, both flat. The bass and violin start up. Rainey takes the two flights of stairs alone to her pink room with the light tread of someone whose fury is as weightless as the air she breathes and gets through an entire side of *Ziggy Stardust* before Tina, looking smug and, at least, embarrassed, appears with a clarinet case.

"Loaner," she says. She looks helplessly around the room, cradling the case in her arms. "Where should I put this?"

WHAT RAINEY'S DOING IN art is developing her métier. Mr. Knecht says every artist has one, and every student must seek one, and Rainey's is making tapestries. She uses everything: cloth, photographs, lists, snippets of lace, buttons, earrings, ribbon, even bits of flat scrap metal. Mr. K lets her go her own way while the rest of Studio Art II makes linocuts.

The other thing she's doing in art, on this bright blue afternoon, is harassing Leah. The girl is carving a face on her linoleum block with a stiff anxiety that dulls her work. Mr. Knecht, oblivious to the hazards of placing two lionesses with a giraffe, has seated her with Rainey and Tina. Tina can't draw well either, but she has the advantage of not giving a fuck. Also, she has the advantage of Rainey, who leans over when Mr. Knecht isn't looking and lightly chisels Tina's linoleum, adding gesture and grace.

Every time Rainey starts to ask Tina to come over, she hesitates; she envisions Howard giving her breathing lessons from behind, breathing being a big deal for musicians. *Breathe from here*, she imagines him saying, his hands over Tina's lower abdomen where—as she conceives the body—clothes tumble round in a hot dryer, and then, sliding one hand up to her breastbone, *not from here*, he would say, and it would be pure Howard to do this, and it makes Rainey sick.

She wonders if she can tell Tina to leave the goddamn clarinet at home. She is afraid that Tina might bring the loaner, swing it insouciantly, like a purse.

"You know what your problem is?" Rainey tells Leah.

Tina looks up from the worktable, interested. She is carving a deer under falling leaves. The deer stands on legs of exquisite delicacy, courtesy of Rainey.

Tina leans across the worktable, threatening Leah's linocut with a sharp instrument. "Yeah, let's discuss your problem," she tells Leah. "I bet I can fix it." Leah raises an arm to keep Tina's gouge off her work but doesn't look up, eye contact being a flammable act.

Rainey puts a restraining hand on Tina's wrist. "Don't," she says. She likes how both Leah and her linocut-girl are desperately in need of *style*. She thinks of Gemma, who arrived at West Tenth Street skittish and grateful, and who slid into a sensuous indolence encouraged and shaped by Howard. "Seriously," Rainey tells Leah, not sure whether she's talking about art or life or both, "your problem is you're afraid to make a mistake."

"You're *helping* her?" says Tina, gouge still poised for damage.

Why not, Rainey wants to say, what have you learned about loyalty, hanging out at my house? She grabs a pencil and draws directly on the worktable between her and Leah: linocut-girl's oval face, the swirling hair. "For Chrissake, would you *look*? We have fifteen minutes." Leah, after a wide-eyed moment, watches the pencil move. "This is shading." Rainey makes rapid straight lines to delineate cheekbones and chin.

"Next you'll be teaching her jazz flute," says Tina.

"Would you relax?" says Rainey. "We're going to give her a makeover. We're going to French-braid her hair. Look," she tells Leah, "mistakes are okay. Look what I did. I hacked it off." She leans forward and lifts a thick, chopped-off hank of her own hair. "If you're afraid of something, do it," she says. That's what Howard tells her, anyway.

"All right," says Leah suddenly. She starts carving cheekbone lines. Rainey thinks, I'm getting good at this acolyte business.

"We could pluck her eyebrows," says Tina darkly. "It only hurts the first time."

"Just braids," says Rainey. "You're both coming to my house Saturday."

"I have to be with my grandmother," says Tina.

"Sunday?"

"Grandmother." Tina chisels a leaf with intense concentration.

"Then Friday after school," says Rainey. "Two hours. Come on."

Leah looks up from a place deep inside her work and says, "Am I doing this right?" It is the first sentence she has uttered to Rainey Royal on an equal footing, and Rainey, with pleasure and surprise, realizes that her powers sharpen when she opens the cage door, not when she locks Leah in. She wonders if this is what her father felt when he first put a fiddle with a piezoelectric body pickup in Gemma's arms. Piezoelectric body pickup, she loves saying that, the way it sounds half high-voltage and half slut.

"Try some crosshatching. But yeah." To Tina she says, "Friday, right? And listen—don't bring the clarinet."

Tina looks at her sharply. Leah drops her head low over her linoleum block, a tumble of red hair concealing her face. Rainey touches her arm and says, "We promise not to be bitches."

"Speak for yourself," says Tina. "Howard told me to bring it every time."

LEAH SITS FROZEN ON the dressing-table stool in Rainey's pink room while Rainey and Tina cross and recross the lengths of hair they're braiding flat against her head. If she's breathing, Rainey can't tell.

The girl has a Renaissance face, half beautiful and half plain. "You look like a Botticelli," Rainey says.

"Andy Sak might like her when we're done with her," says Tina.

Leah winces, though it might be from how Tina combs out each new section with a yank. "Botticelli," she murmurs. "He did Venus on that shell."

"Goddamn," says Rainey. "I should have talked to you sooner. We should go to the museum. Tina won't come with me."

Tina looks over at her. "Yes, I will," she says. "I will, Rain."

Rainey ignores this. Miss Delectable Dial will have to earn her trips to the museum. "Reach over and get her something cute out of my drawer, Teen."

"I don't need to change," says Leah. "Just the makeover."

"This *is* the makeover," says Rainey. "We're hanging out tonight."

"I'm not allowed," says Tina, but she hands over a white blouse that Rainey has altered so it's mostly lace below the bust. She looks at Leah with her hair completely off her face and says, almost to herself, "I don't recognize you."

"I know," says Rainey. "Gorgeous, huh."

Male footsteps make the stairs creak. Tina tends to a new section of braid as if studying an algebra equation in very small print. Rainey listens to the second flight of creaking and waits for the doorway to fill with Howard. On the stairs, he is humming bebop. *Hum job*, thinks Rainey. It sounds half musical and half obscene, a phrase she has heard before, probably in this house.

When Howard appears he is all door. His hair falls to his shoulders in a way that makes women tuck it behind the Kool over his left ear.

"Hi, Howard." Tina's voice is slow and musical, as if everything in the room is under water. Rainey watches her closely. Stolen earrings gleam from under Tina's hair, and on her wrist is Paul's watch, which seems to Rainey like a terrible risk: walking down the street with plunder flashing like traffic lights.

"Miss Temptation." Howard bows his head formally.

"Hi, Mr. Royal," says Leah, and to Rainey, "It's beautiful, but I can't wear it. You can see everything—"

"I wear this to *school*," Rainey says.

"It's Howard," says Howard, "and somebody in this room should definitely wear that."

"Can I try it?" says Tina.

"Not you," says Howard, studying Leah. "Her."

Leah says, "I decline."

Rainey watches Tina's fingernail slip into her mouth. She marvels that Leah thinks everything is about the shirt, when in fact Tina is waiting to be tuned again by her best friend's father's attention, and Howard is flirting with the school giraffe.

"What, do I not get a vote?" says Howard. He uncocks the Kool from behind his ear. Tina rises with a pink plastic lighter, and he grips her entire hand while he inhales.

Then he kisses her knuckles.

Rainey, fierce, says, "Howard, would you get *out*? You got the clarinet vote, that's it. Put it on, Leah."

"Where's the bathroom?"

"Leah, will you just turn around and put on the top before I undo this whole damn makeover? I swear I'll take out every braid."

"Why are you doing this?" says Leah softly, fingering the lace. "I can't change here."

"But you can," says Howard. "I won't look." He turns sideways in the doorway, extends one arm to the opposite doorpost, and tucks his head down behind it, smoking.

"He won't cheat," says Rainey, because she knows this one thing about her father. He likes to win what he gets.

Leah looks at Howard with his head under his wing. Then she scoots around on the dressing-table stool. Her spine is as long and pale as a yardstick, bisected by a white bra strap. When I'm done with her, thinks Rainey, she'll be wearing black. Leah turns back in the mostly lace blouse, and Rainey says through her fingers, "You're beautiful. I bet you had no idea."

Howard turns, too. He presses his fingertips to his lips, then opens his hands wide. The gesture is packed with irony, but Rainey wonders if Leah can tell. Leah is the tottering lamb who cannot see the altar. "Daughter, you have said it. She has no idea. It is the source of her beauty."

Tina doesn't wait for Leah to even blush. "I can't go out tonight," she says, as if she has spent the past five minutes submerged. "You should wait for me."

Rainey looks at the clarinet case. It is a pebbly black box that hunkers by her dressing table. With sugary innocence she says, "We won't go anywhere exciting. Maybe we'll hang out here." She gets a hooded look from Tina.

"Fine," says Tina. "If they play again, I'm going down to listen."

"In that case," says Howard, "why don't we have a brief lesson."

Don't, thinks Rainey.

"Have fun at the *museum*." Tina picks up her pack and the loaner clarinet.

"Always carry your ax," says Howard approvingly. He puts a hand on Tina's shoulder.

Rainey looks away. She senses that Leah, demoted now to merely the girl in the lace blouse, seems altered by what she saw in Howard's eyes. *The source of her beauty.* She sits straighter. She feels, Rainey decides, shinier.

Rainey can be a mirror, too. A better mirror. She will finish the French braids and teach Leah the Pearl Drops toothpaste move, and they'll steal some of Howard's pot. Maybe Leah will sleep over. She will teach her how to dance.

"You should take off Paul's watch," says Rainey.

"You should quit using Estelle's photos in art," says Tina coolly.

"Who's Estelle?" says Leah.

Howard makes an arch in the doorway with his arm. Tina ducks under it without looking back.

THEY ARE, IN FACT, having an actual lesson.

From outside Howard's closed door Rainey hears clarinet scales, clumsy, with mistakes and do-overs. She walks into the bathroom and listens through the narrowly open door. For a moment there's silence from the bedroom, then fluid, mournful scales pour from the clarinet—that would be Howard, of course. She's never really thought about clarinet till now, the way its private, throaty unhappiness underlies even its lighter notes. She thought oboe had sole claim to musical grief.

Silence again, then Tina's laughter.

She listens through ten more sets of scales—Tina's— punctuated by murmurings and bursts of laughter. Lessons should not be this much fun. An ache opens in her stomach and spreads to her chest. From the third floor, Leah calls, "Rainey?" and Rainey makes her own inelegant music, creaking across the floorboards and back up the stairs.

TINA, CARRYING HER PACK and the loaner clarinet, walks to the subway at Union Square and takes it uptown, like crazy far. Rainey watches her from between the cars, swaying.

Leah, still wearing the lace blouse, hangs back. Tina stays on till Ninety-Sixth, where all the white people disappear off the face of the planet. "God, let her walk downtown," says Rainey, but she follows half a block behind as Tina heads north on Lex. They pass Spanish people and tough-looking kids just out of school. Tina walks without apparent fear.

"Are we safe?" says Leah. In fact people are staring at her, a girl two inches shy of six feet, hair braided tight but flaming in color, lace revealing her navel.

"We're cool," says Rainey. Toughness is her métier, but she does not carry a knife like everyone knows kids do up here, so she is feeling a little freaked. She turns her mother's ring around on her finger; now the diamond and rubies won't flash.

"She'll see us," says Leah. "She'll kill me." She considers. "She'll try."

Rainey's not sure who knocks her out more, this pretty shiny brave Leah, born in her pink room an hour ago, or reckless Tina who strolls toward robbery or rape or whatever awaits chicks who wander past projects in Spanish Harlem. Maybe, having held a gun, Tina lost her fears. Rainey certainly feels more capable.

"Let's get this over with." Rainey grabs Leah's wrist, bone thin, and they walk up behind Tina at the light on Ninety-Eighth.

"Tina," says Rainey, and when Tina whirls around, "Don't get mad. You owe me."

"I knew you were there," says Tina, "and I owe you shit. You, you're dead."

"I quit being dead," says Leah, though she looks at Rainey when she says it.

"You're in my neighborhood, you might already be dead." They are standing outside a hair salon with its door open and that Ricky Ricardo music playing. In the window are pictures of women with different hairstyles, fancy ones, updos, stuff none of the Urban Day moms would be caught dead with.

"You're Porto Rican," says Rainey.

"Puerto," says Leah automatically.

"*Tú, cállate,*" says Tina. "Puerto. I ride the bus. Is that a problem?"

Rainey scrutinizes her. "You don't ride the bus."

"Say it. I ride the bus," says Tina.

"But you don't," says Rainey. Tina has dark honey hair and light skin, though Rainey can almost now perceive the faintest cast to it, maybe, she thinks, like Sophia Loren.

"That's your big fat mistake. You look at me, but you don't see. *I ride the bus.*"

She wheels around and walks toward Ninety-Ninth. Rainey and Leah follow. They pass a storefront that fixes flat tires and another that seems to sell dolls covered with dust and has young men lounging outside, watching them intently. "Okay, if it matters that much, you ride the bus."

"It matters that much."

"You ride the bus, and you're going to give me that fucking clarinet."

"I'm going to give you shit."

"Clarinet," says Rainey, "or I never talk to you again."

Tina hesitates, then thrusts the clarinet hard into Rainey's arms. Suddenly it's the last thing Rainey wants to touch.

"Your father is—fucked up."

"Did you kiss him?"

Leah looks back and forth between them, riveted. A meat truck roars by, almost consuming Tina's answer.

"No," says Tina, but she says *no* with two syllables, and Rainey hears *yes* and lifts her hand. Tina doesn't flinch. "He touched my mouth."

"He touched your fucking *mouth*? With what?" Rainey's hand is gripped at the wrist by Leah. She wonders if she would have slapped Tina.

"He put two fingers on my lips. He said pretend it was the mouthpiece. He just said blow. It was part of the lesson."

"Did you kiss them?" Rainey lets Leah push her hand down.

"His fingers?"

"Yeah, were you kissing his goddamn fingers?"

"It was like this, if you really have to know," says Tina, and on the corner of Ninety-Ninth Street and Lexington Avenue, surrounded by passersby and storekeepers in doorways and a boy with a transistor radio to his ear and two young men in suits and a young mother with a baby carriage, she takes

Rainey's first two fingers. Rainey lets her do it, lets Tina put her fingertips with their bitten nails on Tina's soft lower lip. She feels the damp flesh and the hardness of teeth as Tina edges her fingertips fractionally deeper and thinks, *This is the softness inside Tina Dial*, and, a second later, *My father was here.*

Tina closes her lips and blows.

Rainey yanks her fingers back and wipes them on her top.

"I didn't know what to do. He's Howard Royal. He was giving me a lesson. Is that a kiss?"

"No," says Rainey. "It's disgusting. He's my father and you were in his bedroom and that makes you—"

"Go ahead," says Tina.

Rainey looks up the block, where a Dumpster is parked outside a fenced-in empty lot. "Wait here," she says. Because of Howard her mother has split and her best friend has almost defected, and there have been other losses she cannot find words for. She walks to the Dumpster and hurls the clarinet case inside. It lands on a raucous heap of bottles.

She walks back to Tina and Leah and says, "Tell Howard you gave it back to me."

"It's under control," says Tina.

"That's criminal," says Leah. "I could find it a home." She starts forward, but Rainey grabs her backpack strap. They watch in silence as a teenage boy in burnt-orange pants moves in on the Dumpster.

"So you were going to follow me all the way, right?" Tina says. "You almost call me a slut because of your sick father who can't give a normal lesson to save his life. I suppose now you want to meet my grandmother."

"She *exists*?"

"You seriously want to know—forget it." Tina starts walking uptown so abruptly they trot to catch up.

"Why wouldn't she exist?" says Leah, and Rainey thinks, We have to give this girl a job more interesting than being perpetually in the dark.

Tina laughs. "Yeah, she exists." Her voice takes on a caramel edge—that's the only way Rainey can think of it. "The question is, do *you* exist? She thinks I study with a good Catholic girl named Silda."

"You lied about *me*?"

"You think a decent Puerto Rican grandmother would let me hang out at your house?"

Rainey opens her mouth and closes it. They turn east on 101st Street. People gather on the stoops of brownstones in a proprietary way that Rainey never sees in Greenwich Village, and it seems to her that every one of those people ignores her, stares at Leah, the beautiful giraffe, and nods or says something in Spanish to Tina.

They stop in front of a gray building zigzagged with fire escape and crosshatched with window gates. "So, my grandmother," says Tina. "If you look at her funny, your most private business is going to be all over the school."

Rainey feels half like a butterfly has landed on her wrist and half like a knife is angled to her neck. She notices that

Leah, not the type to glance at anyone's grandmother funny, is doing a decent job of staying under Tina's radar. A pack of kids saunters toward them, checking Leah out while they talk and smoke. She wonders if Tina will walk them back to the subway after dark or if they will have to get there on attitude alone, keys spliced out between their knuckles. Or maybe not. Some of those boys are gorgeous.

"She's a sweet lady. I cook her breakfast and dinner, and I try to keep the scholarship you didn't know I had. And I don't get paid twenty dollars a week to live with her, and it sucks that you didn't believe me."

Rainey lights a cigarette. Leah makes a small, shifting gesture, and Rainey passes her one. The pack of kids breaks, swarms around them, regroups.

"It sucks that I have to think about you sucking on Howard's fingers," says Rainey.

"Blowing on," says Tina. "I quit clarinet, obviously. I quit Howard, okay? He's like . . . hypnotic. He's a creep, if you don't mind my saying."

Rainey doesn't mind. "Where are your parents?" she asks.

"My mother and sisters live below us. They're Colón. I'm Dial like my father. So listen, when I introduce you to my grandmother, you say, *Buenas tardes, Señora Colón.* Do it."

Leah bares a long throat, exhales a stream of smoke, and utters the words in perfect Spanish. She's done being an acolyte, thinks Rainey. She had the acolyte tenure of a moth.

When Rainey tries the Spanish, her tongue feels thick.

She wants to touch Tina's hair. It's got strands of light blond in it, maybe Dial blond. "I didn't know you could cook," she says.

Tina shakes her head. "Museum, Jesus," she says, and pushes open the front door. To Rainey's surprise, Leah steps into the lobby first. The floor tiles are laid in a jazzy pattern, and music pulses through one of the apartment doors. Rainey hears trumpets playing faster and brighter than they do in her father's music. She hears quick percussion like the congas in the park, and some fantastic clacking sound that makes her want to move, but she doesn't know how. The pattern on the floor tiles is practically jumping, and Leah thrusts her hands in the air as she follows Tina up the stairs, circling her hips on each step. Climbing behind Leah, Rainey looks up and sees Tina on the first landing do a little two-step, hips held straight, not swaying like when Rainey puts on the Doors. Rainey hopes that if she does everything right—if she repeats the Spanish, if she believes the stuff about the bus—Tina Marie Dial will teach her how to dance.

THE GRANDMOTHER IS TETHERED to earth by the steel wheels of her chair and the absence of one leg. Her remaining leg, and her upper arms, are buttery loaves of flesh. Yet Rainey looks at the high cheekbones and flawless hairline, the elegant ledges of brows and lips carved as gracefully as Tina's, and takes her in as shapely. Someone has pinned up the grandmother's thick silver hair with curved combs, and gold hoops hang from her ears. Rainey repeats to herself: *She has no idea. It is the source of her beauty.*

Clearly not blind, the grandmother looks the girls over, wary and pleased. On the wall behind her is a thrilling picture of a heart wrapped in thorns and encircled by fire. It's clearly connected to Christ, whose portrait hangs nearby and who would resemble Howard if he clipped his beard. *Something something amigas*, the grandmother tells Tina. *Something comida.* Her one foot has lost its curves to swelling, but she wears a neat white ankle sock, folded down at the top; and it occurs to Rainey that the person who washed that sock, and dried it, and put it on, was Tina.

Rainey takes a deep breath and says, *"Buenas—buenas—"* and prays to Saint Cath for the rest. She dips into a little curtsy of desperation as Leah steps forward and says the words.

The grandmother nods once, as deeply as her chins allow. "Beautiful," she says in four appreciative syllables. She might mean Leah or the perfect Spanish or that Tina has brought her these lovely girls from the outside world. Rainey looks at the flames bursting from the heart of Jesus and thinks: For this I sacrifice the clarinet.

I KNOW WHAT MAKES YOU COME ALIVE

Barbie melts slowly, but she melts. She smells like the chemical highway in New Jersey. Her wrist softens to a blackened nub.

Around her the tar paper is marked by dozens of ashy burn marks. Chimneys and ventilation fans populate the roof like random landmarks, and farther out, hundreds of black rooftops quilt the Upper West Side under a purpling sky.

Rainey is spending the night at Angeline Yost's. She squats on the roof with her back against the parapet and watches Angeline's little sister, Irene, burn Barbie. The three girls crouch half hidden behind a chimney in case the super comes. Irene has stripped the Barbie naked and holds a Bic lighter under the left hand.

It is the fall of Rainey's junior year. Rainey and Angeline are friends from music, the only subject that seemed to make

Angeline happy before she flunked out of Urban Day. The Yosts live in a housing complex on West One Hundredth Street near Columbus Avenue with NO LOITERING signs posted at the entry. About fifteen people were loitering on the long, low steps when Rainey arrived—a party, with a laughing baby and an ice chest.

Irene, who is twelve, does not speak. She isn't mute; it is some choice she has made, and it lands her in detention every week—Angeline talks about this with pride. Irene has to burn stuff. It's a compulsion. "If she doesn't burn something small, she'll burn something big," Angeline says. She rises and hugs herself.

Rainey unfolds herself from her crouch, too, not wanting to see the Barbie's hands melt. "That works?" She figures it's okay if Irene hears. It feels important to understand, somehow. "She burns a Barbie so she won't burn down the *building*?" She looks down at the doll despite herself.

Irene smiles at Rainey enigmatically. She has the same straight curtain of hair as Angeline's but a distinct way of ducking behind it. She holds the Barbie gently, almost tenderly, at the waist with two fingers and lights the Bic under the long yellow hair. The flame climbs and flares into a halo around the small, pretty head, blackening the scalp.

"It's like stealing." Angeline looks out over the city and shivers. "You take a bra so you don't take three tops and get caught."

When the Barbie has sacrificed her hair and her hands,

they go back downstairs and close the door to the room that Angeline and Irene share. It's got two sets of matching furnishings standing on curvy ivory ankles. The room gives Rainey an ache, the way everything tries so hard to be pretty. There are twin beds with headboards, a poster of Isaac Hayes taped up above one, Mick Jagger above the other. Irene has Cinderella sheets under her Mick Jagger poster, and Rainey wonders which sister put him there, with his lanky muscles and that lush cup of a mouth.

Angeline gestures at her own bed. "If I sleep under the sheet and you sleep under the blanket," she says, "we won't touch."

Rainey has brought all her drawing materials, in case things get dull, and now seems like a good time to pull them out. The lack of music bothers her. A no-name stereo sits on one of the desks, with records spilling out of their jackets around it. She goes over to inspect. She should pick out a record. But someone has amputated the arm from the turntable, and it lies nearby, sprouting wires like torn nerves. *Stepfather*, Rainey thinks.

She sits carefully on the desk. Angeline flops down on her bed and props her chin on her fist. "So, your dad?" she says. "He's a famous musician, right?"

Irene sits very still on her Cinderella bed.

Since when does Angeline know, or care, about her father? Rainey never mentioned Howard. Tina could have told her at school—except Tina said Angeline was a slut. Angeline copied off Leah in bio; maybe Leah told her. Rainey shrugs one shoulder like Leah does and says, "Semifamous if you're obsessed with jazz. I brought my sketchpad—want me to draw you?"

"What do I have to do?"

"You're perfect. Don't move." She slides off the desk, pulls colored pencils and a sketchpad from her pack, and takes her place next to Irene, but not too close. "Tilt your head toward me. Now open your fist." She sees, beside her, Irene's hands open in tandem. Rainey starts roughing out Angeline, fingers long and graceful despite the chewed nails, eyes focused on some distant place where loitering, Rainey imagines, is a religion.

"So listen," says Angeline. Her words sound blocky, as if she's trying not to move her mouth. "My boyfriend, Jay? He's incredible. He plays guitar. When we sing in the park, people practically *throw* money at us."

It's true that Angeline's throat is a flute. She can do Joni Mitchell almost as well as Joni Mitchell can, and some old blues stuff that Rainey, from her father's Billie Holiday records, knows is the real thing. She steels herself for an audition question. Angeline would be a bowl of cream to Howard, an afternoon's catnip. Rainey is not going to deliver a girl up to her father. It's bad enough that Tina has Howard hypnotized.

Angeline says, "I want your dad to meet Jay. He needs a break."

Angeline's nose is long and elegant. Her hair is dark at the roots, and Rainey draws it that way.

"*Jay* needs a break?" Rainey's reminded of a girl at school who saved up six hundred dollars, God knows how, and bought a color television for her boyfriend. He kept sleeping with other chicks, and now she has razor scars on her wrists. "My dad doesn't give breaks."

This is half true. He's given breaks to lots of young musicians, but there are terms. If one is female, sex with Howard is involved. Rainey can't miss it, and she would like to. Sex with Gordy might also be involved. Always, Howard veneration. Intense amounts of discipline. Personal chemistry.

And jazz.

"Your dad hasn't heard Jay," says Angeline. "He's amazing. We do folk rock. It's a twelve-string guitar, and he writes his own songs. If your father just heard him once, I know he'd do something, make a call—he might even set up some studio time—Jay is *that good*." She smiles a private smile and starts humming something soulful that Rainey recognizes in her veins.

Her fingers tighten on the pencil. She keeps sketching, conscious of close attention from Irene.

"He wouldn't," she says. "I'm sorry."

"Would you look up?" says Angeline. "Please? He might. Musicians like to help other musicians. You could try, right?"

Rainey's pencil freezes. When she manages to get her hand unstuck, she starts adding some visual weight to Angeline's dime-store earrings. "So," she says finally, "you think you'll get your GED?"

Irene's hand moves into her field of vision. Slowly, with her forefinger, Irene traces the outlines of the sketch. She puts her finger to her pursed lips and then applies it to a corner of the drawing.

"Yeah?" says Angeline. "Is she making me pretty?" When Irene nods it is with her whole body, slowly.

After a moment, Angeline says, "What're you, kidding? What would I do with a GED?"

Rainey senses that Irene is straining for cues, or instructions, on how to get through school, get through life. She, at least, has Saint Cath to guide her.

"I don't need school to sing," says Angeline. "We do great. Maybe we'll do greater after Jay meets your dad."

Or maybe Angeline won't even graduate from singing in the park. "My father hates folk rock," Rainey says. "He hates everything that isn't jazz. He won't listen," she says, to clinch it.

"Just have us over," says Angeline. "He doesn't have to listen. He'll *hear.*"

"I'm not supposed to play music so he hears it," says Rainey. "Why Jay, anyway? Why not you?"

Instead of answering, Angeline gets up and walks over to the sketch. "Wow," she says. "I'm taping that up. It's mine, right? You know how many men offer to help me? It's Jay who needs a break." She takes the sketchbook and examines the portrait closely. "I tell you what," she says. "You think about it tonight. And I'll hold on to your book." Playfully, she waves it away from Rainey and slips it under the pillow, as if Rainey cannot reach it there. "Think about it," she says. "I'm just asking to visit you."

Rainey is not afraid to take her sketchbook back from under the pillow, but she would rather not fight with Angeline. So she thinks about it. She thinks about it while they watch television, which she cannot stand, with Mr. and Mrs. Yost. She thinks about it again before dawn, when Angeline turns onto her side and flings an arm across Rainey's ribs, waking her. In the faint light of a streetlamp she sees that Irene's eyes are open. The weight of the arm—possessive, familiar, female—sends Rainey into a state of shock and bliss, as if she suddenly had a sister or a friend so close they were allowed to sleep like this. Tina would never permit it. What if Angeline wakes and catches her tolerating the arm? She thinks ahead to a morning of saying no, of bickering for her sketchbook, of Angeline possibly getting pissed.

In slow motion, she rolls out from under the arm and slithers out of bed.

She tugs her jeans on. She sees Irene watching her silently in the dark, blows her a fingertip kiss, and keeps dressing. She extracts her sketchbook from under the pillow and slips out of the room past Angeline Yost, whose throat is a flute, who has told her: *People throw money at me.* Who has shown her: *Some fires need to be set.*

HER FATHER CONFRONTS HER in the townhouse parlor. "Four o'clock in the morning? Interesting, Daughter."

They have arrived home at the same time. He and Gordy were coming from a club.

Rainey puts her face in her hands. She likes the view better that way, ever since Howard sent the paintings, the chandelier, and the Biedermeier secretary desk to Sotheby's Parke-Bernet, to raise cash.

"You knew I was at a sleepover," she says.

"And what happened, a lover's quarrel? Police raid the party? What sent you out in the street before dawn? No need to hide your face," says Howard. She and her father sit in facing armchairs. "Look up, sweetheart."

Her left wrist smells like tea-rose oil. Her mother trailed the scent through the house until she split, and Rainey still dabs it on every morning, between her toes and on her wrist. She plans on wearing tea-rose oil until she dies, whereupon she will leave instructions regarding the perfuming of her corpse.

From far upstairs comes laughter and music, the *twirp* of Radmila's electric flute.

Rainey sends her softest voice out from between her fingers. It's a voice she's got down. "Gordy," she says, "would you please make me a grilled cheese?" Gordy slides off the sofa arm with ironic obedience and goes into the kitchen.

"Whatever you were doing, don't be embarrassed. We should be talking frankly. Look up, kiddo."

Through her fingers she sees Howard relaxed and smiling, his long body slung diagonally in the armchair. Her father's never touched her—it's her fault she feels so bare in his presence, as if he were smiling and nodding right through her clothes. Relaxed, that's how a chick should be, discussing sex with her father: casually slung.

"For Chrissake," he says, and calls into the kitchen. "Tell her it's 1974, Gordy."

"It's 1974, babe," Gordy calls back. "You have a pretty hip father. Talk to him."

"No one says *hip*," says Rainey.

Howard shrugs. He pats the chair cushions, digs out something that appears to be bothering him—a recorder, of all things—looks at it in a puzzled way, and then toodles on it. It sounds wrong for him. When he stops playing he says, "So tell your old man exactly what you've been doing until four in the morning."

"I was sleeping at a friend's and I left."

"Have I met him?"

"Her."

"If it was a her," says Howard coolly, "I don't think you'd walk out at four in the morning. Not that you have a curfew. I'm not archaic." He walks the recorder between his fingers. "They teach you the important things? How girls your age are approaching a biological peak?" When Howard talks about *girls your age* she wants to smash things. "It's evolution," he says.

Of course he would say this right as Gordy reappears. The plate clicks on the coffee table, and she smells the cheddar. She was starving, but now the smell makes her stomach clench. Far beneath it she smells Howard's sandalwood oil. "Nourishment," says Gordy. His hand moves her hair aside and parks on the nape of her neck. Howard says nothing. "Milk?"

"Coke." Rainey tightens. She wants milk, but she doesn't want Gordy saying the word. The hand goes away. She waits till she hears the kiss of the fridge and takes her face out of her hands. "You're gross," she tells her father.

"Guilty," says Howard. He crams the recorder back between the chair cushions.

"Fuck you," she says, and he laughs as if a child had said something clever.

"You *are* gross, Howard," Gordy says, walking back from the kitchen with Rainey's soda, and in that moment she thinks, *It's only hair, it's only stroking*, and she looks at him with relief.

Her father unslings himself from the chair and goes over to lean against the open piano. He drops a hand in and plucks at the wires without looking, creating an atonal melody that quickens Rainey's breathing and irritates her. The truth is she doesn't like jazz. Howard Royal's daughter does not like jazz. He has tried to teach her about sixteenths and what it means to be on top of the beat or just behind it; he has played her the softly articulated notes called ghosts. But to her, his music has about as much internal rhyme as a flock of birds flapping up startled from the sidewalk.

Rainey thinks about how the lunchroom at Urban Day goes silent in her ears when Andy Sak looks at her across all those tables, stares right past Tina and Angeline, past Leah hunkering over her tray. Forget 1974: he could be any young male out hunting who spots her gathering. Of course if it were a thousand years ago, they would probably converse about as much as they do now. Sometimes she loves Andy Sak and lets him do things and sometimes she ignores him for weeks.

She takes a bite of grilled cheese and propels herself off her chair. "You are such an asshole," she tells her father.

Howard's fingers strum the piano wires, and he laughs. "Welcome to my house, Daughter," he says. "Where I get to be the reigning asshole."

RAINEY CUTS SCHOOL THE next morning and goes to the Home on the Upper West Side where her grandmother Lala lives. It's an emergency. She waves at the front desk staff without signing in. They are all old friends. She takes the elevator to three and walks into Lala's room. They lock eyes and smile their privacy smile. "Look who's here," says Bethie, Lala's private aide, "aren't you a sweetheart," and she moves off with heavy twitching hips to watch the other patient's TV. The other patient is a wispy woman, half paralyzed and mute from stroke who can't complain when Bethie changes the channel. Lala pulls the plastic mask from her nose and mouth and nestles it down around her neck. "Dear heart," she says.

Lala does not know about the sale of the oil paintings and the art deco and Biedermeier furniture. She is *adagissimo*, Howard says. Even Rainey knows that's slow as a funeral. Lala left the townhouse weeping in an ambulette. No one moves out of West Tenth Street the normal way. Rainey's grandfather, Pawpaw, who played jazz trombone, stayed away longer and longer on tour till finally he never came home. He is old and poor in Cincinnati now, still married to Lala on paper. Rainey's mother got into a taxi at dawn, leaving behind her things and the scent of tea-rose oil. And Howard's students depart furious or in tears when he has used them up.

But Rainey, Rainey will never go. West Tenth is hers. The house sits on its foundation and grips the concrete, and she will inherit it when Lala dies. Every time she visits, Lala says it. It is their ritual.

Last night Howard said, *Welcome to my house.*

"I'm making something new." From her pack she extracts the beginning of a sculpture she has wrapped in a pillowcase—a pair of Lala's fancy shoes from maybe the 1950s painted cobalt blue inside and out. She took the shoes from a carton in the basement and has started to adorn them with bits of vintage costume jewelry from Lala's boxed-up things. What she doesn't say is that she plans to glue them to the top of Lala's girlhood Bible, and paint that, too.

"But those are mine." Lala turns the half-encrusted shoes and looks at them from all sides. "Oh, my," she says. "This is about me, isn't it. You're making art about your grandmother." She looks at Rainey with shining eyes. "You know, honey, that house and everything in it will be yours when I'm gone."

So it's still true. Rainey kisses her grandmother's parchment hand and says, "I'll take good care of it, I swear."

Lala used to float through the townhouse like a distracted queen. She wore long dresses the colors of Jordan almonds and beamed at the sexiest acolytes as if she had no idea they were anything more than Howard's violinists and vibraphonists. Her bedroom, on the second floor overlooking the street, looked like the inside of a Fabergé egg. Rainey loved Lala's room. She could never have imagined a time when Howard and his girl musicians would steam Scalamandré wallpaper off the walls, pull the canopy off the antique bed, and take down a French chandelier shaped like a purse.

Lala's bedroom door had certain magical properties. It was as if brass sections in the parlor went mute for her when that latch clicked shut; it was as if Rainey's mother stopped taking the stairs from Howard's bedroom to Gordy's and spending all that time on the roof. It was as if Gordy stopped slipping into Rainey's room to tuck her in late at night.

It was as if Howard stopped living off Lala's money.

Rainey's door, on the other hand, was porous as silk. Horn and piano flowed through it like water. A mother could kiss her, pass through it, and disappear. The door never even registered on Gordy Vine.

"I want Tina to live with me," Rainey says. Tina has never said one judgmental word about the Gordy situation, has never said, for example, *What's wrong with you—just tell him to get out of your room.*

"That's very sweet," says Lala.

"And I want Gordy to leave. He bothers me." She waits to see if her grandmother has antennae when it comes to bothering.

Lala's gaze becomes curiously focused, as if she is examining fine needlework.

"Fine, honey," Lala says. "That's between you and your father. Would you pour me some water?"

"Well, that's the other thing," says Rainey. She pours a cup of water from a pink plastic pitcher and pops in a straw. Lala waves it away. "I want Howard to go, too. If it's my house, I want to be"—she has just heard about this, at school—"an emancipated minor."

Lala struggles upright against the pillows. "Howard is an idiot," she says vigorously, causing Bethie to look up. Rainey makes it halfway into a shocked laugh. "But he is also your father. Do you know what it means to inherit a house in trust?"

Rainey becomes sharply aware of the hum of things: the turned-down television and the blue corrugated tubes that jerk and sigh as a machine breathes into Lala's mask. She imagines the molecular slosh of Lala's pee as it inches along the catheter. The sack of pee, nearly full, hangs dangerously close to Rainey's leg.

"You can trust me with the house." Rainey caresses Lala's shiny nails, which Bethie polishes with opalescent Revlon polish. The image of Saint Cath, folded at the bottom of her pack, radiates light. "The house will save my life," she says. With Tina as backup, Rainey might be strong enough to make Howard and Gordy move out. At least the acolytes and folding chairs would have to go.

Her grandmother says, "Howard is the trustee. He lives there. He buys the heating oil; he pays the taxes. If he sells the house, it's for your benefit. For college, say." Her grandmother smiles and closes long, crinkly eyelids; she looks sleepy. After a moment she says, "A girl needs a guiding hand till she is twenty-five."

At twenty-five she'll be watching Sotheby's Parke-Bernet cart away the floorboards; they have already taken so much. She drops her grandmother's hand. It creeps back to Lala's breast like a daddy longlegs.

The gray day, through wet windows, leaches fluorescence from the room. Rainey suppresses a childhood desire to chew on her hair.

"You know he auctioned off the chandeliers?" she says.

Lala's fingers interlace and stroke one another as if they were seeking comfort.

"You know he sold the Biedermeier secretary?"

Bethie drifts over. "Stop upsetting your grandmother, honey."

"Does she look upset?" As far as Rainey's concerned, Lala has closed the bedroom door in her head. "She's fine."

"I don't know," says Bethie.

"He'll be a lousy trustee," Rainey says fiercely. Heating oil she figures she can live without, and taxes—she is sixteen, who is going to make her pay taxes? "Make me the trustee, Lala."

Lala's breathing becomes shallow. "Howard is your *father*."

"I warned you," says Bethie. She sashays to Lala's side and pulls the mask back over her mouth and nose. Lala and the machine breathe in slow harmony.

"Howard is an asshole," says Rainey.

Bethie's entire body takes on the attitude of one who has been slapped.

"Dear heart." Lala, breathless, lifts the mask. "Howard is only trustee of the house. A girl must always be her own trustee."

SHE TRUDGES TO THE subway. She murmurs it. *Be trustee of her own self; be trustee of the house that is her person.* She steps, distracted, onto the IRT local. Don't confuse the house of her self with a parlor once lit by a chandelier—a room where plaster cherubs now hold hands around bare bulbs and watch over her from wide, dusty eyes.

Her father has instructed her as to her assets. Among her

debits: like most Americans, she hears disharmony when she listens to jazz. It is a failure of ear, imagination, and heart. "Though at least you're not one of those people who says"— his voice rising into a falsetto—"'Oh, play me something,' and then talks right through it."

THAT DAY AFTER SCHOOL she stops at the hardware store to explain about her door.

"You need a shim," says the man, and shows her a thin, splintery wedge of wood. "Take it," he says, pushing back her quarter. She can only get the tip in under her door. That night she goes to bed with the light on and stares at the doorknob. At around 1:00 A.M., the knob turns.

The door does not move.

The knob turns twice more. Then it stops.

THE NEXT MORNING, JUST showered, Rainey opens the bathroom door. Her mother's bathrobe is red silk with a wine-dark stain on the belly, and has a deep V neckline, and things look a certain way on Rainey. She could wear a laundry bag and make it look good; her mother has said it.

But Gordy, who leans against the banister outside the bathroom, white hair fanned out around his shoulders, does not appear to have laundry bags on the agenda.

"Do you mind?" she says, hanging back. He could be waiting for the bathroom, but she doubts it.

"I got your message last night," says Gordy. "And I respect

it. I respect it. But let's not act so aggrieved that we have to bar the door. All I ever do is say good night." No one else is moving in the house. They keep their voices low.

Rainey crosses her arms. "Say good night when," she says.

"You know when."

He says it as if he were citing the grilled-cheese sandwiches. Sandwiches she eats. Sandwiches she is complicit in.

"You come in my room when I'm sleeping?" From the way he looks at her, she knows they both know that she knows. She waits for him to laugh at her. "Don't you dare laugh," she says.

He doesn't laugh. "You have no right," she says. She pulls back her hand and slaps him on the face, to see if it will relieve her of the horrible knowing feeling. It does, a little, though her hand must be burning at least as much as his cheek. His skin turns bright red. She wonders if he is really albino or just incredibly pale. He makes no move to slap her back.

"You sent me signals," says Gordy. "You've sent me signals your entire life."

Signals? She sends signals to everyone, all the time, even if the signals are submerged, like telexes in cables on the ocean floor. It's what she *does*. It doesn't seem to be something a person can learn; Leah is hopeless at it.

Gordy raises his elbows to block her hand. "You never said no." He backs up toward his bedroom door.

Two flights down, the doorbell rasps. "You weren't listening," says Rainey, and shoulders past him and downstairs.

She opens the heavy front door to find Angeline, Irene, and a guy with eyes like polished black stones.

"Are you *Jay*?" She's aware first that the high autumn sun is rendering her red silk robe translucent and second that Irene is holding the burned Barbie, scorched at the ankles and wrists where it is missing its hands and feet. "Sweetheart, you can't bring that here," she says.

She senses Howard before she sees him beside her in his tartan pajama bottoms, breath minty, hair wild. "Is this the boy?" Howard's chest and abdomen are bare. His beard needs trimming. She hates doing it.

Jay straightens and says, "Yes, sir."

"You told him." Angeline leans in and squeezes Rainey's arm. "You'll love Jay, Mr. Royal. We didn't wake you, did we? It's after ten."

"I don't have to love Jay." Howard scratches a sworl of hair below his navel. "All that matters is if my daughter does."

"Your daughter?" Jay looks at Rainey as if she is the real reason he has come. "We were hoping," he says, and stops.

"So you'll listen?" says Angeline.

"To what?" says Howard. His gaze locks onto Irene and then on what she is holding. "I'd say you were too old for dolls, gorgeous, but you play rough." Irene smiles uncertainly. Howard laughs and turns. "I'm going back to bed."

"Daddy, wait." Rainey can't help eyeing the Barbie. Irene smiles at her and holds it out. Rainey shakes her head. Howard's at the stairs. "Daddy, can you wait just *five minutes*?" she calls. Howard waves at her without looking and climbs. "Three minutes? For me?" Howard is gone.

"Goddammit," says Angeline. "You promised. You promised and then you ran out on me." She strides past Rainey into the foyer and looks into the parlor. "If we play right here, will he hear us?"

Irene sidles past Rainey into the foyer, too, but Jay stays outside, holding his guitar case and looking at Rainey in the doorway, and she's looking at him, too, the way his eyes gleam like fountain-pen ink, and his mouth looks hard and soft at the same time, and his chest tapers with elegance and economy. They only have seconds of staring in which to make up for all those years in which they have been strangers to each other.

"I know where you live," he says finally, meaning he can come back alone to see her, but for a moment Rainey thinks he means *I know what makes you come alive*, and she thinks, *Yes, you do.*

"Come in and play," calls Angeline, but Jay doesn't take his eyes off Rainey.

"It won't do any good," he says. It's a question.

"No," she says. But she steps back so he can come inside.

Then, shocking herself, she shouts out to Angeline: *Sing.*

Angeline moves out of the parlor doorway.

Rainey watches her ascend to the third step and look up toward where Howard disappeared. She hears her voice, sweet and slow and big-throated, aching and full of blood like a heart. Angeline sings "Cry Me a River," and her voice swells the staircase. She keeps singing, and it draws Howard slowly to the banister and down a few steps from the second floor in his pajamas. Angeline sings, and they all stare at her, Howard from above, and Irene sitting on the bottom step with her neck craned, cradling the Barbie, and Jay and Rainey in the foyer. Jay holds his guitar case in one hand, and his free hand is near Rainey's, and she can feel his fingers laced in hers even though they aren't touching.

Then he moves past her, sits on the bottom step by Irene, takes out his guitar, and picks at the strings. To Rainey's amazement Howard sits, too, at the top of the stairs. Gordy pads down from his bedroom and leans against the wall behind Howard.

Angeline's voice is invisible and everywhere; it is seawater that rises through the rooms. When she stops, the silence shimmers and contracts. Rainey would like to draw her now, in triumph, her breastbone high, her gaze aimed straight up at Howard like a light. She remembers the weight of Angeline's arm across her chest.

Howard waits a few moments and claps his hands together slowly three times.

"Very pretty," he says. "You should sing in the park. Try some open mikes. You'll do very well."

"That's it?" Angeline stands marvelously erect.

Rainey reaches down, smooths Irene's hair, smiles at her, and gently pries the Barbie from her fingers. The scalp is black, but the eyes are bluer than sky.

"What did you expect?" Howard rises. "You have to grow into that voice, my sweet. Live a few more years. Have your heart crushed."

Rainey sees him wink.

"What about Jay?" says Angeline.

Irene looks at the floor.

"Jay will always be your accompanist," says Howard.

"I told her we shouldn't have come," says Jay to anyone close enough to hear.

Angeline is still staring up the staircase at Howard. "Screw you," she says softly, and her shoulders droop.

Howard beams down at Angeline. "Anytime."

Jay is suddenly busy with his guitar case, and Rainey wonders if he will be staring at her again. Howard yawns and turns.

Rainey perceives Irene's fingers closing into fists, and she tightens her own grip on the Barbie. She feels the seam of a hip printing onto her finger; she feels a tiny, fulsome breast pulsing into her palm. She feels the doll's skin heat in her hand.

"You don't know how to listen," she calls, then flashes on Howard attending to Tina's scales, on a clarinet lesson behind a closed door. "People throw money at her," she shouts, as Howard disappears up the staircase. "Some girls are better than you think."

BABY GIRL

Damien's curls sweep Rainey's face. He smells of last night's communal dinner: chili with red onions and Cabernet. He clamps her mouth with his right hand and fastens her wrists with his left. He lives above Rainey in the former servants' quarters and is a student of her father's; he could wring blood from the cornet, Howard says.

Damien's in her room because she slid the shim out when he knocked. He was upset about Howard. He's on her bed because she drew her feet up for him to sit. At three o'clock in the morning, to talk. Just to talk.

She would never scream in her own house.

She feels like pieces of her body might be falling off, like turrets and bell towers from a castle. Damien stops, finally. He peels his hand gingerly off her mouth. Her teeth hurt. "Thank you," he says, and zips. "Fuck, you're magnificent." She spits at him. The spit lands on her quilt.

"You are *on the street*," she hisses as he ambles toward her bedroom door.

With a hand on her doorknob, he turns. He wears a plain white T-shirt with a hole at one shoulder and lanky jeans; and under these he is thin and taut as a wire hanger. "Why?" he says. "Why would I end up on the street?" He has a look of serene entitlement, Rainey thinks, as if, having nothing extra on his person, he feels he can take what he needs.

"You patted your bed," Damien says, already half outside the pink room. "You did that thing with your eyes."

When she hears him on the stairs, she bolts down to Howard's room. Her father refuses to turn on his lamp. "Talk," he says wearily. She stands in his doorway in her nightgown, which Damien tore at the top, and hears a second body stir under the sheet.

"You have to throw Damien out right now," she says, wondering which of her father's acolytes is listening under the covers. "Please, can I talk to you privately about this?"

"We're one family," says Howard. "And we're all asleep."

"He just forced himself on me." She knows she is backlit by the stairwell light, which she has switched on, and she holds the top of her nightgown together in one hand. "I am not joking."

"Damien? My beautiful boy?" From the rustle she can tell he's propped himself on an elbow and is peering at her. "I wasn't awakened by screaming."

"Daddy. He had his hand over my mouth." And it is true that she fought, but it is a lie that she tried to scream. She wonders if Damien is already asleep.

"Oh, Rainey. Oh, baby girl." Howard switches on his lamp and the light washes his face. To Rainey he looks ravaged by exhaustion and also, to her surprise, deeply sad. She locks eyes with Radmila, the Yugoslav flautist, who holds the sheet to the butter knives that are her collarbones. Radmila gives Rainey a tiny, apologetic smile.

Howard has not called Rainey his baby girl since she was a child. It is the winter of 1976, and she is seventeen years old and feels like she is five, standing before Howard with a dead sparrow and asking him to make it fly.

"It sounds like something went very wrong, baby girl."

"Will you throw him out?"

"I'll give him hell. I guarantee he won't touch you again. He won't even look at you on the stairs. Will that do?"

"No," says Rainey.

Howard rakes his fingers through his hair till it stands. "Ah, Jesus," he says. "Have you heard that boy play cornet? Have you *listened*? An artist can't be a criminal. Listen. Young men get confused about yes and no. I wish girls could understand that."

"Men get confused about a lot of things," says Radmila. Rainey looks at her sharply, but there's no smile.

Howard, half covered by the blanket, pins Rainey in the doorway with his gaze. "How did Damien get into your room?" She is silent. "So you let him in," says Howard. "Could that be half a yes?"

Rainey fingers the rip that Damien began. She will finish it when she gets back to her pink room. She can hear the sound already, long and zippery. When she gets to the hem, she'll rip the gown the other way.

"Rainey. Did you let him sit on the bed?" Rainey says nothing. "Could that be another kind of yes?"

"I don't know," says Rainey. "I just know what happened."

"If I talk to him right now, will I see fingernail gouges on his face?"

Radmila says softly, "Howard. She said he forced her."

Howard lies back with his hands under his head. "I believe there was rough play," he says. "I'm so sorry you were hurt, baby girl. Can your father offer some perspective?" The blanket jumps as he scratches a calf with his foot. "Can I?" he says gently, as if she were still waiting with a limp bird. "Radmila, don't you need a glass of water?"

"Why would I need a glass of water?" says Radmila.

"Because you're dying of thirst," says Howard. "Go." Radmila shrugs, gets out of bed naked, picks up Howard's T-shirt from a chair, and puts it on. When she has slipped past Rainey and started padding downstairs, Howard says, "When I was a boy, my babysitter—"

"I don't want to hear this."

"Oh, you can tell your old dad about Damien, but I can't tell you my story? What is that? Listen," says Howard. "I was about nine, and she got me all mixed up about sex and pain and whether I could walk away. Sex, if you can call it that, went on for two years. Crazy, huh? So I know exactly how signals get crossed."

Rainey squints, trying to keep certain images out of focus. "There was no signal," she says. "I told him we could talk."

"Maybe he misunderstood your cues," says Howard. "Maybe what you are experiencing now is called regret."

He reaches over and palms something on his nightstand, and Rainey hears the tiny tambourine sound of a pill bottle being shaken.

"Regret?" says Rainey. "You think what I'm experiencing now is called regret?"

"Sweet baby girl," says Howard, "take a Seconal. Sleep. Tell me how you are in the morning."

Rainey does not take a Seconal. She closes the door. Magnificent. Howard's beautiful boy has said it. Magnificent is how she will be in the morning. She walks up two flights of stairs to Damien's tiny room, bangs his door open so it shudders on its hinge, and turns on his light. "Sit up," she says, as he blinks at her from the narrow bed. "You have to listen to me."

She will stand on the townhouse stoop, the flaps of her torn gown open. Snowflakes will rise beneath the streetlights. Cold air will scrub her clean.

KEEP MY HANDS FROM STEALING

Rainey locks herself into the ladies' room of the Madison Gardens coffee shop, not far from the Met. It's perfect: a little bathroom for one. She slings her heavy pack over the doorknob and pulls out a glass pillar candle she decorated herself for Saint Cath.

Lights the candle, wobbly on the sink, with her last cardboard match. Strips off the T-shirt she stayed up all night in. Slicks under her arms with soap.

Cath, I need five minutes in this grotty bathroom. She slips a plastic razor from a pocket of her pack. *You can do that. And let old Mr. Lipschitz love my work, and let him maybe give me a place to live and let him have, like, zero libido.*

She shaves the left pit. Someone rattles the knob.

Rainey cruises through the right pit, leans over the sink, and washes her hair with the green bathroom soap. This is what she wants Mr. Lipschitz to smell: soap and tea-rose oil. Not leather jacket and sweat. Not that she left the townhouse unshowered at five in the morning after a fight with her father, who had just returned from playing a gig.

Last night she found an older girl sprawled on her pink bed, making actual jazz come out of Rainey's junior-high flute. The girl's enormous duffel was propped against the dressing table. This kind of shit was always Howard's doing. Rainey's eighteen, but this girl looked halfway into her twenties. She wouldn't leave, so Rainey waited up for Howard till almost sunrise. He came home with an arm draped around Reba, who had bongos between her legs in Union Square till Howard lured her indoors.

His fingertips dangled low.

"The casa's a little full, sweetheart," he said when Rainey demanded her room to herself. "Grab a sleeping bag. Or duke it out." His middle finger brushed Reba's nipple, and a spark flew out and caught Rainey in the eye.

The knob of the ladies' room turns again. Rainey has an interview in twenty minutes—she looked at the restaurant clock—with an old man who might commission a tapestry.

"Hang on," she says. She ties a turquoise scarf around her wet hair and slicks Vaseline on her eyelids and lips. Shine, she loves shine. Men have eyed the shine on her since she was a kid. They are, all of them, so full of shit. But this is not a problem she would bring to Saint Catherine of Bologna. Cath scorned temptation and the worldly state. She was all about the art.

Loud knocking. "Hello, there are three of us out here?" Rainey had cut ahead of a lady in slingbacks, and right through the paint-chipped door she can see her, how her hat matches her gloves. On the Upper East Side it is the hour of church; it is the hour of brunch. Rainey skipped dinner, and she is too broke for breakfast. And she's forgotten her perfume.

Without perfume she's stripped of her powers. She passes her wrists quickly over the candle flame, prays, *Saint Cath, anoint me. I make you all these pretty things.* It's true, Cath could perfume her own flesh from molecules of nothing, a miracle she performed after death instead of rotting, and Rainey believes she smelled of tea rose, the scent of mothers.

New knock. Male. Some serious knuckle in it.

"What?" she says. "I'm not feeling too well."

Brilliant—in a coffee-shop bathroom, not feeling well means junkie; it means needles jamming the plumbing. She swipes on deodorant, lifts one foot to the sink, starts dry-shaving her leg—and accidentally rocks the glass-pillar candle. It falls with dreamlike lassitude, then explodes. Shrapnel everywhere.

Hard banging, and a male voice. "Whatever dope you're doing in there, sister, you got five seconds before this door opens."

In five seconds she opens it herself. She's wearing a low-necked, gauzy black tee on which she's painted the face of Saint Cath in gold. *Be resplendent*, she thinks. Glass parings glitter at her feet. Her lips part. Her eyelids shine, and she stares at the manager. His eyes flare with a look that needs one of those long German names that would mean something like anger braided with lust.

"Scram," he says.

He reaches for her arm, and she tries to wrench away, but he escorts her past a line of staring women and out into the sun.

FROM THE LIVING ROOM of the Lipschitz apartment, she hears a door close far off with a chocolaty thump. She hears footfalls that speak of Persian carpets. It's Fifth Avenue. To get this far, she's been scrutinized by two doormen, an elevator man, the housekeeper.

The man who limps into the room is thin and angular as a branch snapped off a winter tree. His eyes are ice blue. He catches her in deliberate scrutiny of a little Impressionist landscape hanging by a grand piano—as bare as her father's, which she knows better than to even brush against. She's chosen the landscape because it hangs in a place of honor. "You're the artist?" he says in some kind of accent.

She forces herself not to brush invisible leaves from her skirt, takes a measured half second to tear herself from the painting, and beams at him. He holds an ebony cane topped with a silver dog's head whose nose thrusts through his fist. He's dressed up—a suit, a tie. Church and brunch again, though with a name like Lipschitz, who knows about church.

"I brought a sample of my work," she says.

She opens her army pack, which in this peach-colored room has all the presence of a burlap sack, and pulls out a white satin bag. The bag is cinched shut with a black grosgrain ribbon, voluptuously tied, and holds something the size of a gallon of milk. She cradles it in two hands like an offering, and waits. Inhaling, she smells tea-rose oil wafting from her wrists. Cath is restoring her powers.

He looks at her with startled gray eyes as if surprised to find a girl in his apartment, wet hair trailing down as if she'd walked in from the sea.

"Vonnie Gardner says you want to take a scissors to Eleanor's things," he says.

But he knew. He asked her to come. He saw the tapestry she designed and sewed for his friend Mrs. Gardner, and examined it a long time where it hung on the wall. Mrs. Gardner wrote this to Rainey in a letter, which she found stepped on in the West Tenth Street foyer. Mrs. Gardner wrote that Mr. Lipschitz seemed to examine aspects of her late husband in all the intersections of the tapestry, in the buttons and fabrics, in the photograph fragments stitched down with gold thread, in the cuff links and snippets of shirting—collar points and even buttonholes—worked with exquisite neatness into a pattern of Rainey's own devising. Rainey loves patterns, she loves kaleidoscopes, she loves butterfly wings arranged in mandalas under glass, and she loves rose windows in cathedrals, all the intricate designs of nature and man that make a closed system.

"Allen looked at it so long," Mrs. Gardner wrote, "I offered him your name. It took him a while to understand that I was talking about memorializing Eleanor."

Rainey's stomach makes an inappropriate noise.

"Mr. Lipschitz," she says, "I won't cut up any materials you don't desire me to use." She lets the words *desire me* hang in the air with the dust motes, but they don't seem to register. "This is a tapestry I made for another gentleman. May I open it?"

She follows him into the dining room, extracts the rolled-up cloth from its white silk sleeve, and unfurls it on a table of inlaid wood: her pattern on his pattern. Mr. Lipschitz stands near her, lean and old and elegant in his black suit.

Rainey wonders what that fine, dark wool would look like in a tapestry. She never says *memory quilt*, though she thinks it. She says *two months, roughly*, and *five hundred dollars*. When the right moment comes, she will ask to work where the beloved lived. If the person is rich, she might ask about an extra bedroom. If the person is rich and lonely, it can be a balm and a novelty to have a young artist stay.

RAINEY KNOWS THE SECRET of stepping very, very close to a man without actually moving her body, and she does that now. She sniffs: he smells nothing like an old man, rather a bit like eucalyptus. Eleanor must have chosen it. She wonders if he is aware of his own patterns: the mosaic of book spines behind glass doors; a bracelet of landscape paintings circling the room. Around the table, the backs of dining chairs swoop and curve in heartlike shapes.

The tapestry, which she borrowed back from a widower on Park Avenue, is less than a yard square but heavy. It's made from a few hundred diamond-shaped cuttings of florals and pastels. Prints spiral loosely down the center, while solid colors stream toward the edges. Rainey does all her sewing by hand—she tells people the feel of the fabric helps guide her through the work—and this is true, but it is also true that her mother's sewing machine is broken. At many points where the diamonds of fabric meet, she has stitched buttons, pearls, the face of a ladies' watch freed from its band and glass, an Eiffel Tower charm, a tiny key, a Victorian locket, snippets from old photographs, their edges pierced by the points of the finest needles.

But it is the center of the piece that draws the eye back: part of a small wedding photo in black and white. She has carefully torn the edge to deckle it and sewn it to the tapestry using mouse-stitches.

"Your wife's tapestry might be simpler. It depends on what you tell me about her, what's in her closet and jewelry box."

"And I would do with it what?"

"It's a work of art. It hangs on the wall. You look at it and remember. If it were me, I'd light a candle in front of it."

Mr. Lipschitz fingers one of the pearls.

"It's good you're doing that," she says. "They get dull if no one touches them. The oil on your fingers makes them glow. Did your wife wear pearls?"

He pulls his hand back.

"A Yahrzeit candle you light once a year, Miss Royal."

Lighting a candle once a year, that's nothing. When they dug Cath up after two and a half weeks and found her body still resilient, the nuns took her home to the cloister, cleaned her up, posed her in a chair, and lit candles at her feet. Five hundred years of nuns lighting maybe a million votives— that's devotion. Not this Yahrzeit thing.

"Or you can just look at it and remember her," she says. She needs a cigarette. She needs a sandwich. She needs a shower with fluffy white towels. "Do you want to see photos of other work?"

"What I want." He takes a seat at the head of the table. "I want something beautiful like this to give our daughter. Something filled with Eleanor."

It sounds like a yes—she's hired, right? She's sure she's hired. *Cath, I owe you majorly.* Maybe it's why he wore the suit: to meet the artist, to seal the deal. Around her the floorboards gleam darkly, framing ornate rugs.

"Mr. Lipschitz," she says. "I forgot to eat breakfast."

"Who forgets to eat?" He picks up a little bell by a crystal candlestick and rings it, and soon after inquiring what she might bring, a woman in white sets down a tray holding a sandwich and milk in a delicate glass. She looks like a nurse. Rainey almost faints with pleasure.

"Thank you," she says, "for trusting me with your wife's things. I promise you won't—"

He puts his hand up. "I get it already. Eat. What do you need from me, to do this thing?"

The sandwich is roast beef with thinly sliced cucumber. The bread has no crust. It is divine.

"I need to choose my own fabrics and objects, though I'll never use anything you want to save." She waits. "That includes some jewelry," she says, and waits some more. "And I prefer to do the work in your apartment. If you can accommodate me." She does not yet say *feed me*. She does not yet say *live in*.

He rises like someone presiding. He's in good shape for an old man. No gut, and no cane when he doesn't feel like it. "Miss Royal," he says. "Five hundred dollars I understand, but Vonnie Gardner let you work in her apartment?"

"Actually, she let me stay there. You'd be amazed how much that helps." It was, in fact, incredibly peaceful at Vonnie Gardner's, like a hotel room where you had to behave. She waits to see if Mrs. Gardner ever mentioned that in the third week she caught Rainey hanging halfway out the bathroom window smoking a joint, which Rainey persuaded her was an herbal cigarette. Mrs. Gardner made her leave the spare bedroom, though she let her keep working days at the kitchen table.

"Where are the parents?" says Mr. Lipschitz.

Where are they how, she wants to ask: emotionally,

geographically, sexually, what? She knows how to smile and talk at the same time, and she does that now. "May I have another glass of milk?" she says.

He rings the bell again, and the woman in white, whose hair, Rainey now sees, is captured in a net that is nearly invisible, inquires and returns with the glass, which is so thin Rainey is afraid to hold it. When she's finished, Mr. Lipschitz leads her through the kitchen to a small white room, simple and scrubbed clean. *Without sin*—Cath would have loved it. Twin bed, white headboard. A small white bureau. One window facing a brown brick wall. Serene and slightly shabby like the barren rooms once meant for staff and now inhabited by acolytes at the top of the West Tenth Street townhouse.

"It's beautiful."

"Beautiful," says Mr. Lipschitz. "Tell that to the maid. The maid would rather live in Queens."

The walk to the next bedroom takes them past closed doors and old photographs and bookshelves and art. The hallway seems to keep unrolling. Rainey waits for him to stop, to turn slowly around. Sometimes, after standing too close, men remember the shine on her skin; they smell the tea-rose oil, and it drives them mad. And she *wants* to make them feel these things, and she wants to hold them off. It's a delicate balance. It's a constant calibration.

But Mr. Lipschitz does not turn to her until they arrive at a large, square bedroom, with windows full of park and sky. He steps back so she can enter alone. The walls are upholstered in

cornflower-blue silk—she touches it, walking in—patterned
with swallows and leaves. Underfoot is a blue rug she wants
to curl her toes into, and the bed has a blue silk canopy, too,
gathered and radiating out from the center. Rainey is doing a
different kind of calibration now. She is thinking yardage. She
is thinking the fabric and workmanship on the canopy alone
could have bought her a year of art school. She is thinking
Mr. Lipschitz should adopt her.

"Is this where your wife slept?"

"You wanted to see her things, I'm showing you her
things."

"What I meant was," and she strokes the padded wall. "If
she slept surrounded by this fabric, I wouldn't mind incor-
porating some. If you had extra somewhere."

He shrugs. She lets it go.

On the bureau is a black-and-white photo, the old kind
that's nearly sepia, of Mrs. Lipschitz: dark eyed and with a
generous mouth, from about a million years ago. "Boy," says
Rainey. "She was gorgeous." He looks at her oddly. It's hard
to miss. "May I open the bureau?"

"Suit yourself." He watches from the doorway, holding
his ebony cane.

She's made eight of these tapestries for clients. She evokes
the dead through fabric and bits of jewelry, and she is good
at distilling the heart of a person to a tight and complex pattern. The people who hire her are old, and some have aides
or furs or wheelchairs or little dogs. She can't understand

what it feels like to be widowed, and they can't understand her work till it's done.

Five hundred dollars for two months' work sounds like a lot of money, but it never lasts.

Saint Cath, please guide my eyes, she prays, *and keep my hands from stealing.* She has to pray her prayer, or things from good people end up in her pack, and she hates that about herself.

In the first drawer she finds two old, skinny watches with little square faces. One has diamonds embedded: she won't ask for that, but watch faces are highly desirable, detached from their bands—they can always be reset if the owner has regrets. She puts the watches on the bed in their little white box. She rubs her fingers over vintage slips frothing with lace and an entire drawer of silk scarves in zinnia colors, as if packets of seeds had burst into bloom in the dark.

Mr. Lipschitz moves into the room. He looks like a crow, perched on a dressing-table chair.

"May I?" She waits for his shrug of permission and opens the closet. It's almost a room, for heaven's sake, with a tiny chandelier and rods hung one above the other. The clothes are arranged by color like a formal garden.

She turns to him with a broad smile. He makes a spreading gesture with one hand. *Take what you like.*

Mrs. Lipschitz left the planet without her black wide-brimmed hat, which might yield three speckled feathers and a cutting of felt. She abandoned a black velvet riding jacket and a cream bouclé suit. She gave up a trove of cashmere sweaters, which Rainey raids for their mossy texture, and blouses in fabrics that will swoon to her shears: challis, Egyptian cotton, silk charmeuse.

Rainey steps out with her arms loaded up. Mr. Lipschitz is gone. She lays the clothes on the bed and looks at Eleanor Lipschitz's blue jewelry box. It has a key sticking out. Jewelry is sensitive. Better to handle it in front of people. She checks both ways down the carpeted hall. "Mr. Lipschitz?"

She runs her hand over the box.

No one's ever left her alone with jewelry. Mrs. Gardner sat down with her husband's cuff links, many of them gold, asked worried questions about how Rainey planned to use them, wept, handed a few pairs over, and seized them back. She could not relinquish them till she'd talked awhile. Now twelve cuff links wink from Leonard Gardner's tapestry like stars in a stained-glass sky.

"Mr. Lipschitz?"

She opens the box, standing to one side so that everything she does is visible from the doorway, and begins laying out the contents around the photo of Mrs. Lipschitz.

Of course there are pearls. With women there are always pearls. But Eleanor Lipschitz owned two strands more different than Rainey has ever seen.

For an Eleanor of propriety, a double strand of white Cartier pearls lies crisply in a red silk case.

For a darker, perhaps an artistic, Eleanor, a long string

of heavy, misshapen black pearls snakes and clicks in a gray suede bag.

Was she one person at night, and one by day? Rainey covets both necklaces. He will have to sacrifice them. Or parts, at least: Rainey can take a handful of pearls, and the rest can be restrung. This daughter of his may want everything for herself, but the tapestry will not be honest without both Eleanors.

Still waiting for Mr. Lipschitz, she folds the clothes from the closet and arranges everything by color on the bed, the black pearls snaking across an apricot sweater and the white pearls glowing against rose. She wonders if her job has already started and what she will cut into first. She loves her scissors. She has a pair of French sewing scissors that cost almost twenty dollars, and a pair of adjustable couturier shears that can cut through multiple layers of fabric and would have cost nearly fifty dollars if she hadn't slipped them into her purse and run.

No one comes, not even the lady in the white dress.

She picks up the riding jacket and holds it up to herself in the mirror. It is beautifully lined and constructed. It makes her hungry all over again.

"Eleanor." She tastes the name. If she says it fast, it sounds prim, like the white pearls, but rolled in the mouth it is sensual, brooding, like the black. She takes a longer look at the photograph. In the picture Mrs. Lipschitz looks about eighteen. She looks, in fact, much like Rainey herself would look if it were the sepia age, not 1977. No wonder he stared at me that way, she thinks. The young Mrs. Lipschitz has the same straight dark hair and narrow face, the same chiseled eyes that might be half Chinese. Her eyebrows are high and arched, as if faintly surprised, and her gaze is intensely focused on something seen only by her. This was not a chick to go all soft for a portrait. She is sexy, despite the high-buttoned white blouse, and she seems to sense her own powers. This gives rise to a familiar feeling that Rainey finds sustaining.

I know her. Black-pearl Eleanor. *I can make her tapestry.* The hall is still empty. She slips the riding jacket over her hand-painted T-shirt and stands before the full-length mirror. Even with Converse on, she looks sharp.

"Eleanor." She rolls the name in her mouth, unties her scarf, brushes her still-damp hair with Eleanor's hairbrush, and puts on the feathered hat. *Très* glam. She works off her sneakers and slips her bare feet into Chanel pumps, the exact kind that Lala wore.

Whatever you like. That's what his gesture meant. She holds the black pearls to her neck.

If she were Eleanor, she would wear the Cartier pearls on her wedding day. She would marry a lean young man named Allen who had the world's ugliest last name, but it would be okay because he wanted to protect and cherish her. He would not make her feel small by quoting Shakespeare in a snide and belittling way like her father does, which seems a wrongful use of art anyway, and when he felt lust it would be in—oh, what does she mean? *Context.* It would not just be that lupine thing. A few years after the wedding, when she falls for the black pearls on a Tahitian vacation, he will hesitate and say, *You're not serious, Eleanor? They're full of lumps,* and he will wonder who, deep inside, his white-pearl wife really is to be moved near tears by a strand of what look to him like a bunch of dark, fat, shimmering beans. It will give him a left-out twinge he can never name and never forget. But being Allen Lipschitz, he spends the thousand dollars. *To protect and cherish.*

The sensation around Rainey's neck is cool and satisfying. Her neck belongs to her now; that's for sure. The parts of her body meet at lines as clear as the boundaries on gas-station maps.

From the doorway he speaks low as if not to startle her. "Don't take them off."

Startled, she struggles with the hat and pearls. "I've never—I'm not—" And it's true, she's never played dress-up before, and she's not stealing anything right now, and these seem like ridiculous things to have to say.

"I mean it," he says. "Show me."

She lowers the necklace and picks the hat up off the bed. "Don't be mad. Her things are so beautiful."

He looks at the photo and back at her, a little wry. "There is a resemblance."

"I know," Rainey says slowly. "That's why I did it." It's a small lie, but if she keeps going, it might become the truth.

"I thought if I could see her in the mirror, if I could *feel* like her, it would help me work. Really, I'm sorry."

"The profile. Let me see."

She makes a quarter turn. Mr. Lipschitz stays where he is. Of course if he comes any closer, the mirage might vanish.

"The skirt is wrong."

"Wow," said Rainey. "I know. Are you saying you want me to—you won't flip out?"

"Also the shirt. Fix it. If you will."

She takes a sharp breath. "Okay," she sings, and steps into the walk-in closet, pulling the door behind her.

Eleanor had lined her closet with white silks at one end, black at the other; peach sweaters here, and scarlet there. It would have been easy to dress in the morning if you woke each day knowing who you were. Rainey can't imagine such confidence. She wakes each day having to harden a new shiny case around a grain of sand. Today she will be Eleanor of the dark hands, see how old Mr. Lipschitz reacts. She steps into a slim black skirt and puts on a rose silk blouse unbuttoned to here. The black pearls she slips inside the open collar, so he'll glimpse them, rolling tidelike in and over her bust, every time she moves. She changes the Chanel shoes for a pair with higher heels.

You're dressing for games, she warns herself. But games seem to be her particular gift, games and the art. She never asked for any of it.

Rainey steps out, gives him a bright smile calibrated to

lightly engage, and confronts the mirror. She really does look like the woman in the picture, though the woman in the picture wears her good-girl blouse. Suddenly Rainey feels entitled to ask for things. She turns to Mr. Lipschitz.

His gaze sweeps up and down her body, but to her surprise it lingers on her face. He seems to be searching for something. She can almost feel his throat constrict.

"The hair is wrong," he finally says. "Can you pin it?"

She hopes he isn't forgetting about the tapestry and the five hundred dollars, but this is interesting. Presumably this Eleanor had a normal mother who braided her hair and tucked her in at night. Presumably this Eleanor never felt like her father was smiling at her through her clothes. She stands straight so he can see her figure—it's clear from the photo that Eleanor Lipschitz had that happening, too—and braids the damp strands slowly, planning to twine them around and coil them up. Mr. Lipschitz consumes the small movements of her fingers. She bets he loved watching these little rituals.

She doesn't mean to talk, but it comes out. "My mother used to braid my hair." This is true—she remembers slim, quick hands working behind her, and her mother's thin soprano—but it is also true that Linda hated the detangling that came first and finally abdicated the whole post-bath scene, which then fell to the solicitous Gordy. He would put down his trumpet as if there were no job more important than combing the wet hair of a little girl, inch by tangled inch.

After which he would smooth the hair down her back again and again with his fingers before the braiding could begin.

A tiny sardonic laugh escapes her nose.

She better watch it; she might break the spell.

"Will you put on the watch, please, Miss Royal? No—the diamond watch."

The watch glitters like it wants to get Rainey in trouble. Her grandmother Lala once had a watch like this. Her father probably sent it to Sotheby's Parke-Bernet, with the chandeliers.

"Is it too much"—Mr. Lipschitz sounds like he has a piece of cracker in his throat—"to ask you to sit in that chair and look out the window?"

Is it too much? Is it too *much*? To sit at a window, like Eleanor, who got to keep her blue room? She takes her seat in a blue armchair, leans forward, and looks down at Central Park. She watches a lady steer a baby carriage into a playground with pyramids and stop at a green bench. Mr. Lipschitz lowers himself onto the edge of the bed. Rainey feels herself studied, though not in the way she is used to. Under his eye she feels like an object of great beauty. She senses rather than sees his gaze stop at her glittering wrist.

"A wedding gift," he says.

It seems better not to speak. A faint scent clings to the rose silk blouse. She leans back as she thinks Eleanor might have, arranging herself for a photographer, and fingers the dark pearls as if her mind were elsewhere. She knows her

bust is stunning, and she knows she has this in common with
Eleanor. Once she glances at Mr. Lipschitz—Allen—and
quickly away. It is an intimate act, the way he's staring at her.
Or maybe he is staring past her, at the edges of her, to blur
the image so the similarities sharpen.

Finally he says, "Use anything you want except the jewelry
and watches. They are my daughter's. I'll talk to her. The
maid will give you a key."

With help from his cane, he stands. But instead of leaving,
he sets the cane on the bed. His palms turn toward her, helpless. Around them the room has deepened almost to sapphire.
She feels a curious desire to slip the black pearls back into
their dark suede bag and clasp the white strands around her
neck instead.

"Miss Royal."

"I need the pearls." She rises to face him.

He lifts his hands very slightly; she sees the tremor of age.
"Miss Royal."

"I need the pearls to make the tapestry."

"One time," he says. "For one minute. Never again."

"Not *all* the pearls," she says carefully. "Your daughter
can remake the strands from what's left. But your wife is in
those pearls."

She looks at him, both bent and straight, elegant in his
suit, his body spare. His face is wrinkled, but his eyes shine
dark and frank. He wants something physical, which makes
her wary, but he does not precisely want *her*.

"Think about it," she says, and goes to him. She puts her arms loosely around him. With his arms he encircles her waist lightly, as if they were about to dance. She holds him so only their shoulders make contact and smells his clean, eucalyptus scent, and he allows the side of his head to touch the side of hers, and she wonders what it must have felt like to love this man. Like living in a sanctuary, with a steady supply of roast-beef sandwiches. Is it true there is infidelity in every marriage, as her father once said at one of her parents' parties? She would like to think that he is wrong as she stands in Mr. Lipschitz's arms. They hold each other tentatively but firmly. Their letting go, when it happens, has a slight resistance to it.

Closing his eyes, he thanks her.

"Wait," says Rainey.

Mr. Lipschitz sways. Rainey takes the ebony cane from the bed and puts the dog head in his hand.

She could give him something from Eleanor, right now. She moves piles of clothing from the bed to the floor and lies down, kicking the high heels off. "Okay," she says. Mr. Lipschitz seems deep in meditation, as if studying the floor through his eyelids. "You can lie next to me if you want," she says. She can't say *in my arms*; instead she says *for a little while*.

He opens his eyes and stops swaying. "Miss Royal," he says, "I don't want any nonsense."

"I hate nonsense," says Rainey. "I hate nonsense more than you."

He sits on the edge of the bed and unlaces his shoes. His socks are tissue thin and look expensive and clean and have no odor. He lies flat on the coverlet beside her and looks at the canopy as if he were offering himself up to death.

"Ellie," he says.

"Allen."

"Allie."

"Allie, give that artist girl my pearls."

"Please," he says. "You look like her. You don't sound like her."

She takes his hand.

Silence blossoms under the blue-canopy sky. Lying beside him, on her back, Rainey feels his skin cool and dry in hers; she feels the elegant length of his fingers, his knucklebones in their little sacks of flesh. She finds the warm wedding band and rotates it, and he lets her. She senses the molten glow of the black pearls from the pile of clothes on the floor. In her mind she begins Eleanor's tapestry. It will be bright around the outside with floral colors, but the center will be a full, shadowed moon of dark fabrics: the woman's private, lunar self.

"My wife had a faultless ear for piano," he says, still looking up at the canopy. "If she heard it, she could play it."

Rainey turns on her side so she can see him better. When their eyes meet he closes his. Is he embarrassed, or preserving the illusion of Eleanor? The lids are faintly blue, and when she touches them, her fingertips detect the darting motions of tiny fish.

"She played chamber music three days a week," he says, as if her fingers were not on his eyelids. "But we had our daughter, Joan. I said, *A mother does not work.*" He clasps his free hand to his forehead, headache-style. "She never played again."

Rainey looks around at the cornflower silk. She will razor some cuttings off the back of the curtain hem, where nobody will see.

She moves closer and puts her head on his chest. His heart beats with astonishing persistence. She had thought he would smell something like Lala, who traveled in an envelope of powder and old age. Does he pick up the scent of Eleanor's blouse? She rubs the ancient-looking hand. His skin slips easily across the tendons. She examines him closely. Beneath the surface of his face she perceives the outline of his skull.

"Ellie," says Mr. Lipschitz, "You remember Friday nights?"

"I think so." She sees his eyelashes gleam.

Rainey blinks rapidly. What is there to cry about? She thinks hard about things that will happen next. She will eat roast-beef sandwiches every day at noon and drink milk from a glass nearly soap-bubble thin. She will finish the tapestry before Mr. Lipschitz, too, leaves this planet empty handed. Every morning she will light a candle to Saint Cath in her white room, and some afternoons she will wear Chanel and sit in the slipper chair, watching children at the pyramids in the park. On the blue coverlet, for Allen Lipschitz, she will be memory, and she will be flesh; she will be eighty, and she will be eighteen.

He opens his eyes. "How should I feel?" He murmurs it almost to himself.

Rainey kneels above him without letting go of his hand.

She looks down directly into his beautiful striated irises and lowers her mouth, which is dry, very lightly onto his. Their lips and tongues do not move. Their gazes connect, and with no nonsense whatsoever they hold quite still.

After about ten seconds she straightens.

"You should feel good," she says. "I think I'm ready to start."

TWO TRUTHS

Late-summer Sunday, two years after college: Leah runs into Rainey Royal outside a coffee shop called Eat Here Now. "Friend or foe?" says Leah, delighted with how jocular this sounds, which makes her realize she is still afraid of Rainey.

She watches nervously as Rainey arranges herself against a parking meter. Rainey's whole body seems to smile at Leah with perfect white teeth.

Does she remember upending Leah's purse over the toilet? Or pressing a square of paper onto her tongue and calling it blotter, so Leah stuck a finger down her own throat?

"Friend!" says Rainey. Smile so cocky, voice so velvety— Leah wants to be in her thrall again.

But she has to be at work ten minutes ago; mice are waiting to be injected, though God knows they're in no rush. They're doing Bad Science in the lab this summer, worse than last year. This is where she's worked since she graduated from Amherst. Leah always knows the time, but she looks at her watch. "I'm late."

Rainey catches Leah's wrist. Her grip feels hot, cool, alarming. Leah wonders if she can get her to touch the other wrist, balance her out. "Nice watch," says Rainey. Surely she sees it's just a man's Timex. "Was it your father's? Am I right?" Leah feels herself smiling at the glittering sidewalk. "It radiates dadness. Smart gentle dadness. Same with my father's watch," says Rainey, and Leah feels herself studied as if for small cues. "I can always tell what emanates from a thing," says Rainey. "I work with objects that belonged to the dead."

"That is so romantic. Objects of the dead. I'm jealous," says Leah. Of all the kids from Urban Day, only Rainey could claim something like that. Leah remembers the things she made in art from handwritten scraps and her grandmother's dancing shoes and bits of cloth, while all Leah could draw were lines as straight and clean as her own spine. How did Rainey *know* things, she wanted to ask. How did she *make* things? What was it like living in that Raquel Welch body and having a father who flirted with his daughter's friends? Back when Leah had no boyfriends—not that she has boy-friends now—Howard Royal would look at her like she was standing naked on some shell.

"My job is so gross I can't even tell you. Good-bye," Leah sings out, and starts to wheel away—this is meant to be funny.

Rainey hangs on to her wrist. "C'mon, let's do breakfast. I want to hear about your life." Leah shakes her head. Half of her wants her wrist back, and half of her wants Rainey to hold it all morning. She sniffs. Rainey smells like roses. That hair, too, past her waist, untrimmed, the way it gleams and swings. And that thrown-together gypsy look, as if Rainey somehow lived out of that enormous army pack, scavenging gold hoops and silky scarves from its pockets.

Rainey tips her head and smiles. "Please?" With her free hand she starts to toy with one of the many zippers on Leah's lucky leather jacket.

Leah feels the moment snap. So must Rainey, because her expression freezes. She releases Leah's wrist and Leah's whole self relaxes. Rainey turns her attention to her pack. "All right," she says coolly, "then buy a T-shirt."

Since when does Rainey sell T-shirts? Anyway, Leah's a leotard girl. She likes things trim, tucked in; she likes hospital corners and folded socks. Her mother the decorator has been after her to come to LA and work with her. You know how to position a thing with regard to the space around it, she says. You have restraint. Everything else you learn.

"I don't wear T-shirts," says Leah.

Rainey says, "Then just *look* at one. They're beautiful."

It has now been twenty-four hours and twenty minutes since the last injections: not good. These things should be exact. Rainey unfurls a black top from the pack. It bears the face of a saint painted in gold, a delicate female face with full parted lips like hers and a halo of feathers. She's wearing one like it, with a halo made of little gold arrows. If it were on a leotard, Leah would grab it. "Twenty dollars," says Rainey. "She's pretty, right? She's the patron saint of artists. Look, it's signed."

"It's beautiful, but—"

"But what? She's the patron saint against temptation, too, but that doesn't seem to be your problem." Rainey laughs.

Leah wants to duck; she feels as if a helicopter rotor is whirling overhead. "I don't have any extra money."

"Why *extra*? Don't you ever just buy a shirt? Or a piece of art?"

Leah does not buy pieces of art. She likes her walls bare and white. Her mother has taught her all kinds of decorator facts, such as Things That Should Be White and Every Room Needs a Touch of Gold.

She steps back. "I have to work," she says. "I'm the only person in on Sundays."

"Well, that's cool." Rainey rolls the T-shirt back into her pack. "I'll go with you. We can play Two Truths and a Lie. Then you can help me sell shirts in the park."

"I can't bring you to *work*." Rainey would be repelled by her job, or she would bring mischief into the lab, or both.

"Why not? I'll be good. I won't touch a thing."

Two Truths—whatever that game is, Leah's not giving up any truth. Her truths would be mortifying, and she can't cough up lies. "I'm not allowed to bring people," she says.

Always been obsessed with you. That would be true. *Wanted to be like you. Wanted to have a cruel streak and secrets and a sex life and be an artist.* Is that six nuggets of truth or one big lump? By then Rainey will know Leah is not worth her time. That, or she will attach herself to Leah in some dangerous manner.

"Really, I can't," says Leah.

"You're the only person there," says Rainey. "Who's going to know?"

SHE STROLLS RAINEY PAST the security guard, who knows her and is busy with the *Post*, into an aging, hospital-like building. It's so silent most Sundays, if she stands in certain spots, she can hear air molecules crash in her ears. *Brownian movement.* She loves that. No one works weekends but a handful of lab techs engaged with animals, and they are all on different floors. Monkeys, dogs, rodents, cats.

Rainey looks around as if she has never seen anything resembling a hospital.

"Look, this could make you sick." Elevator goes so slowly. "I have to inject twenty mice who have tumors under their skin. It hurts."

She gets a skeptical look that she takes to mean: It doesn't hurt *you.* "Is that the first?" says Rainey. "Truth or lie?"

"It's science," says Leah, by which she also means, but cannot say: *It is my religion.*

She can't tell that to her mother, either. Helen called last night from LA, where she is becoming known for her highly textured, all-white interiors, to say: That job is sucking the life out of your life. Or words to that effect. Words like: Twenty-three—darling, don't you want a boyfriend? You need some life in your life, darling, besides those fucking mice.

Her mother said *darling* the same way she said *fucking*: so it rang, high and sweet, like a struck glass.

"I like the mice," Leah had said. "They're sweet."

THE DOORS GLIDE OPEN on an old, greenish hallway. Even under fluorescent tubes, Rainey's dark hair shimmers. Leah shortens her stride so she can watch the hair lap against Rainey's back. The hallway leads to a glass-walled corridor where a sign reads BREAULT ANIMAL RESEARCH FOUNDATION. "BARF," says Leah. Rainey looks at her sharply. "Acronym," Leah says happily. At the corridor's end she unlocks the prep room for her lab. It's a surgical space, which pleases her. On the long countertop, she takes bloods once a week from mice she tucks under a bell jar with an ether-soaked rag. Above the counter, a sliver window runs the length of the room. September sun slants through the glass, and she wonders if Rainey, being an artist, appreciates the cool aesthetic of it all: steel cabinets, steel countertop, the scalpels she forgot to zip up in their case.

Rainey ignores a wheeled chair, caresses the slope of a bell jar, and sits on the counter, skirt drawn over her knees. "What do you do in here?"

"Preparations," says Leah. "It's a prep room." No way will

she tell about the bloods—the way she cuts off just the tip of a mouse's tail, the tiniest southernmost slice, and milks blood into a test tube. While remembering to breathe, lest she faint. Mouse is out cold, after its skirmish with the ether. And the tail tip, resembling a clotted pimple, gets flicked into the trash.

Nor will she tell Rainey what had her kneeling, her first day, in the hall, sinking through a lake of algae-colored tile and praying no one in a white coat would walk by. It was the sound: the click of scalpel against the countertop, at the bottom of the slice.

She gathers syringes from a cabinet and, from a lab fridge bearing a sticker that says NO FOOD, little bottles of halothanadol and two Baby Ruths.

"Chocolate?"

"Fat," says Rainey, and grabs some minute amount of flesh at her waist.

It would be delicious to stare. Leah doesn't. She arranges everything, including the Baby Ruths, symmetrically on a steel tray. "I'm on the sugar diet," Leah says. "My theory is it keeps you wired, and you stay thin from always moving."

"Sometimes it's good to be still," says Rainey. "Are you sure you want to hurt those mice?" She taps an unlit cigarette as if she means to light it. In the prep room. Near the *ether*. Leah can't help thinking that she looks like a butterfly in an operating room—a rare and beautiful contaminant.

"Not that I'm squeamish," says Rainey, and tucks the

cigarette behind her ear. "Tina showed me her cadaver in med school. She was dissecting the hands. It was rather beautiful. She said she felt gratitude, not disgust. If you were wondering." Truth or lie, Leah thinks, she's on a roll. She notices the cabinet door still open, syringes exposed. Hoping Rainey won't take it personally, she strolls over and locks the cabinet.

Across the hall she juggles tray and keys, opens the door to the colony, and flicks on the light. The room always feels like a cruel trick. Inside, tall metal racks hold dozens of bare, transparent plastic bins that slide in and out like drawers. Each mouse lives alone in its own bin. And that's it. No daylight, no running wheels, no little shelters, no toilet-paper tubes to scurry into, no cellmates—and mice like to play; they are social and curious. The colony breaks her heart. Some of the mice rear up in what Leah takes to be interest when she walks in. Then they drop back onto their feet, being morbidly obese—literally, genetically, bred that way.

Leah watches Rainey take it in, look around at the bins and sniff. Lab perfume, Leah calls it: fur, food, and cedar. Mice groom themselves, though it's hard to nibble one's own back if one weighs the mouse equivalent of three hundred pounds.

"Sorry, guys, it's us." Always greet the mice. Leah sets her tray down on a metal trolley, which she covets, along with a tower of plastic drawers. *In five hundred words or fewer, explain why you wish to pursue research in the biological sciences,* the grad school applications ask, and Leah wishes she could write about lab equipment, the way its chilly elegance clicks with her brain. So exquisite, how everything in BARF is pristine and performs some precise function. Perfect job for her. Stopping a study because it hurts a few mice is not high on any lab's list.

"They're adorable," says Rainey. "Are they nice?"

"They're gentled from birth." Leah goes to a rack of mice that are not in use and slides out a drawer. "Let her sniff you," she says. Rainey dips a hand in the bin.

Leah plucks her first mouse, Experimental No. 1, a.k.a. Big Handsome, out of a drawer by his thin pink whip of a tail and sets him gently on a scale on the cart. She makes her obeisance: "Yea, though you walk through the valley of the shadow of death," she says, picking up a syringe, "thou shalt fear no evil, for it will all be over pretty soon."

"That sounds awful." Rainey's voice is a texture Leah can't name: water, gravel, silk.

"It's important," says Leah. Halothanadol turns fat mice into thinner mice, that's the general idea. If it can cure obesity, it might cure the side effects—heart disease, diabetes, like that.

"Just say you couldn't do it." Rainey separates out a twist of her hair and dangles it into the bin. "Two Truths and a Lie," she says. "You first."

"Rainey, not now." Leah sinks a syringe through the rubber stopper of a halothanadol bottle, pulls up the plunger, holds the syringe up to look for air bubbles, and flicks it sharply to dislodge them. Then she ejects a fine spray. Big Handsome patrols the perimeter of the scale in little spurts.

"Me first?" Rainey has the mouse in her palm now. It quivers and sniffs. It is the size and shape of a fig. She folds her arm against her chest and lets the mouse creep to her elbow. "I fell in love with an eighty-year-old man," she says. "I was eighteen. I lived in his apartment. I wore his dead wife's clothes, and I slept in his bed. I really loved him."

Leah thinks: I could never make up something like that. She palpates Big Handsome, who might as well be stuffed with tiny pebbles. His tumors are hard, and everywhere.

"He didn't believe me, though. He wouldn't make love to me."

Maybe he couldn't, thinks Leah. Then she decides Rainey is too beautiful to sleep with an eighty-year-old man. She tries to lift some of the pebbled flesh and stick it lightly: subcutaneous, should be easy. Needle hits something hard under the skin. Everything is hard under Big Handsome's skin. It's revolting. She yanks the needle away and releases the mouse, who bolts across the cart.

"Lie," says Leah breathlessly.

"You have to hear all three first," says Rainey. "Or how will you know? Your turn." To her credit, she hasn't gotten sick. Leah looks up, drawn by a small movement, and sees Rainey open a second drawer and take out another mouse.

She tries the shot again, jabbing harder. This time some of the halothanadol gets into Big Handsome, who squeaks and whirls, and nips her finger. Lab mice rarely bite; they're trusting creatures. "You don't want to keep doing that," Rainey says. "Nasty drug."

"It's not the drug," says Leah. "It's the alcohol we dissolve it in. It kills the flesh."

"It'll kill your karma," says Rainey. "Try dissolving it in water."

"You mean saline. We can't. It floats on top, like baby powder."

Leah sucks on her finger and starts chanting in her head because her fingertip hurts, because she deserves it, because she doesn't know if she should give Big Handsome another half shot, because she has nine experimentals left to inject. *Nam-myoho-renge-kyo*, she mutters. Once she read that in Buddhist labs, they don't throw dead mice out in Hefty bags. No, they hold little mouse funerals with incense, and they chant. Send the little rodent souls off in peace. What lie can she offer that will sound like a truth? What truth can she offer that will sound like a lie?

"Go, Leah," says Rainey. "Truth or lie." The two mice waddle up and down her arm, sniffing each other as they pass.

Leah blurts it. "I'm still scared of Tina Dial." She works off a piece of fingernail with her teeth and returns Big Handsome to his plastic drawer. "I know that's dumb."

"Yeah, well, Tina's intense. But you ought to confront it. You ought to see her."

"I'd rather not." She takes out a second mouse.

"Don't take any shit from her. It would be a good exercise." Rainey Royal is looking at me, thinks Leah. "I'll get you together," says Rainey. "You'll be friends. Tina's fantastic. You going to damage that mouse, too?"

Leah sets Miss Mouse delicately on the cart. She calls all the boys Big Handsome and all the girls Miss Mouse. Miss Mouse whiskers the edge of her universe, the metal rim of the scale. Leah writes down her weight, grabs her, and jabs fast. Same horrible squeak. Leah lets go just before she bites. Good for her—she *should* bite. Another halfhearted shot, too. Halothanadol drips from the syringe and dampens her fur.

In five hundred words or fewer, please describe what interactions in the biological sciences, professional or personal, have affected your desire to work in the field.

I like being alone with the mice, thinks Leah. I like the absence of interaction. Though she is jealous of Tina, going to medical school.

"This is awful," she says.

"Don't do it," says Rainey. "Let's set them free."

"They can't survive in the wild. They'd starve." It's a pointless argument. This is her *job*.

"It's New York," says Rainey. "There's pizza crust every-where."

"They're prey. They'd get eaten."

"It's an honest death. Look at you, Leah," says Rainey. "You're shaking." Amazingly, she tucks both mice in the pockets of her skirt. Then she walks up behind Leah, takes her crazy red hair in her hands, and strokes it into a ponytail. Leah can't believe it. Talk about needing to stand still sometimes. This might be the gentlest thing she's experienced at Rainey's hands, and Rainey has, at various times in high school, French braided her hair, slapped her in the face, taught her to dance, and tried to instruct her in numerous things, including some inviting manner of moving the tongue across the teeth that doesn't look like dislodging crumbs, and—there is no polite way to say it—an intimate skill involving an elongated fruit. Leah was hopeless.

"You're a wreck," says Rainey. "You'll never do all those mice." She coils the hair into a twist and tucks it into a bun.

"You've stolen two laboratory animals," says Leah. She can't move. She feels Rainey tuck in one last strand of hair.

"Truth or lie. Remember that cape I wore in high school? I still have it." Rainey steps back. Leah does remember; she remembers even the double line of stitching on the hem, and how the hem sailed out behind Rainey's boots and flapped back to kiss them. "I stole it," says Rainey. "From a stranger. It was the worst thing I ever did."

"That's the worst thing you ever did?"

Leah deposits Miss Mouse back in her drawer, looks at the next mouse, and hears a tiny whimper that turns out to be her.

"Do a mouse and tell me a truth," says Rainey. "Or don't do a mouse. This is a terrible job. You need to quit."

Leah gently plunks Experimental No. 3 on the scale. He scurries and sniffs. "I once locked myself in the prep room," she says, "and inhaled the ether."

"You? Interesting," says Rainey.

Leah doesn't reveal the rest: that in a brief suspended state she saw her father, dressed in bizarrely mismatched clothes, in a corner of the room. He seemed not to see her. He looked around as if watching tiny planets spin in the air, and she thought about the days in ninth grade she'd go from school to the hospital and then home, where she'd clean her room from a chart she made up, so that her furniture smelled of lemon oil and renewal. She was thirteen years old, and she couldn't stop him from dying, but she could vacuum her rug and polish her desk and line her books up like teeth. She remembered all that, sprawled on the floor.

She's been afraid to commune with the ether since, but she wants to see her dad.

Leah strokes No. 3, who looks over the edge of the scale and ponders the cart. There's not one place to slip in a needle.

"It's over, right?" Rainey has taken the mice out of her pocket and strokes them, watching her.

Leah has seven more experimentals, plus the ten controls, who get plain alcohol.

"You mean quit?" says Leah. She looks Rainey in the eye for about five seconds, then has to cut away. She did everything Rainey told her all through high school. Surely she is stronger now. "I can't screw up this way," she says.

"So don't screw up this way," says Rainey. "Screw up by setting them free."

LATELY LEAH'S BEEN DREAMING of torrential rain. One dream she's under a narrow, dripping awning, sheltered by the thrilling technicality of a single inch. Another she stands behind a waterfall, stares through the downpour, dry by the grace of a few degrees.

You can always come work with me, darling, her mother said. You have an eye.

She's been tempted to ask what her mother thinks all this water means. Helen Levinson has theories, sometimes. But Leah would have to explain how good it feels, this thin sliver of safety. She'd have to explain her strange place in this recurring wet dream: arms outstretched, ready to leap.

WITHOUT WARNING RAINEY SETS her two mice on the scale. Suddenly a cluster of identical white mice—faintly yellowed to be exact, pink of tail and inner ear—turn circles around each other. It only takes one second to lose track of Experimental No. 3, and that is the second in which Leah looks at Rainey in shock.

"You just ruined an eight-week scientific experiment."

"Aren't you relieved?"

"You don't understand," says Leah, breathless. "They'll make me sacrifice those mice." She's never been called upon to kill a mouse. Ether overdose, she'd probably use. She's heard of techs who break the tiny spines with a pencil.

"Sacrifice? To the science gods?"

THEY WALK WEST TO Central Park, mice sliding and scrabbling in a cardboard box that once held ether cans.

"Third truth or lie," says Rainey.

"No more. I just stole twenty mice."

"Twenty-two. And you freed yourself," says Rainey. "Here's what I think. I think the ether and Tina are true. I think we'll end up at your place drinking the Jack Daniel's I have in my pack."

"Oh," says Leah, and flushes.

"All true? Am I right?"

Leah nods. She should have lied. She should make some excuse about her place being a mess; that could be her first lie. She's never had company yet—she wears her life too tight. Her favored company tends to be her own chattery, sardonic mind.

They approach the park under a brilliant afternoon sun. Tree leaves glitter when they shiver. Rainey's hair stirs and falls in the breeze. "You haven't guessed mine," she says.

"Both lies," says Leah. "I think you cheated."

"Both true."

"No," says Leah. "Stealing a cape is not the worst thing you ever did."

"It is at gunpoint," says Rainey. "You could turn me in, and I'd go to prison."

Leah inhales sharply but says nothing. She steps more lightly on the concrete as if Rainey's truths were made of glass and she were trying not to crush them. She doesn't ask questions—she finds she likes the not-knowing and the yearning sensation that goes with it. They enter the park and follow a curving path. After a while they walk on the grass and stop at a spot with bushes and a bit of distance from people out enjoying the day.

"This is your baby," Rainey says.

Tonight the mice will be picked off by cats and owls. Still, they have today. Leah opens the flaps and tips the carton. Mice tumble out. Some have dark stains on their ivory fur from sliding around in their pellets. Their noses go right to work, vacuuming. It's like they can't wait to learn about the world. Leah thinks she knows how they feel.

Earth, the noses report. *Grass, moisture, squirrels, dogs. God, freedom, ants.*

"We'll sell a couple of shirts," says Rainey, as if she's just thought of it, "and then we'll go to your place."

She kneels to watch the mice, and Leah squats to do the same. They are close enough for Rainey to lean on Leah briefly, close enough for Leah to panic. Close enough for Rainey, possibly detecting the shift, to straighten. Far enough for Leah to think: *Come back.*

This is going to be complicated, she thinks.

The mice don't disappear at once; they have nothing to run from; they are gentled. They percolate across the grass, edge under a nearby bush, flicker slowly away. There is so much for them to sniff, and the directions they take are so random. Rainey doesn't stir. After a while Leah's ankles ache from crouching.

They wait without moving till the last tail blinks out of sight.

ALL THEY HAD TOGETHER

At Eighty-Ninth Rainey waits as Leah presses her nose to Schatzi's window and sighs over three tall Styrofoam cakes.

They are wedding cakes, frosted with plaster, for all Rainey knows, and a fine, gray dust. The center cake is governed by a plastic bride. "I could eat the whole thing," says Leah. The plastic bride is shorter than her groom, who holds her hand. Leah is nearly six feet tall, and Rainey wonders if she's ever held anyone's hand.

Sweetheart, the plastic groom will say, and the word will hum like a transformer. The plastic bride will take off her dress and lay it on the neighboring cake.

"If you want one, get one," says Rainey.

"You can't just buy a wedding cake," says Leah.

Three weeks have passed. No police ever came. Leah works in a rat lab way uptown now, at Columbia Pres, where they took her references on faith. She and Rainey are wandering back in a relentless drizzle from the museum to Leah's sublet.

Rainey's cigarette hisses at the sidewalk and drowns. "You can do anything you want," she says, and strides into the bakery.

Inside, a shopping cart drips on the terrazzo floor. Empty shelves ache for their lost loaves: it's almost closing. The counterwoman moves slowly. Box, bialys, Danish, string.

"How much is a wedding cake?" says Rainey.

"Oh, my God," says Leah. "I can't believe—"

"Such rain," says the counterwoman, pulling a green pad from her smock. Her hair is teased. She and Rainey will never understand each other; this is clearly a woman who keeps a plastic bonnet in her purse. "How many?"

"One," says Leah. She bounces up and down on the tips of her toes.

"How many *people*."

"Not many," says Rainey. "The smallest you have. But three tiers."

The woman traces a cake in the air. "Four inch, eight inch, twelve," she says, and glances past Leah at the streaming window. "Seventy-five dollars."

Rainey glances at Leah, who is biting her lip. "Do it," she says.

"Oh, my God," says Leah. "Seventy-five dollars for a *cake*. It's a sin."

"For filling," says the counterwoman, "you want raspberry, buttercream, ganache—"

"Buttercream," says Leah, with feeling. "And smooth fondant icing."

"Yeah, and we have this one request," says Rainey. "Instead of flowers—" Many words can be uttered in a bakery, but *mouse* turns out not to be one of them. "The bride is a scientist. She works with mice. Can you do mice?"

"Not on wedding cake."

"Why not?"

"Because five years old," says the woman, "a girl starts dreaming about her wedding, she wants flowers, not mice."

Rainey tugs the woman's pad across the thick glass counter and draws a Beatrix Potter creature. "Look," she says, pushing the pad back, "it's cute."

"I know what looks like a mouse," says the woman. "I have traps. I put day-old bread, the mouse sniffs—" She scurries two fingers across the glass, then slams her palm down.

So, flowers. Rainey asks to have it for the weekend. The woman looks at her as if the cake might be used for some practical joke. "Tina will love this," Rainey says. Leah says nothing, but Rainey sees her tap the glass case. Three left, three right. Rainey puts her hand between Leah's shoulder blades and rubs her on the back.

THE WEDDING CAKE, DELIVERED Saturday to Leah's East Eighty-Third Street studio, is half illusion. The tiers pretend to rest gently on one another, but no. They're set on card-board circles, which are held up by tongue depressors, clipped and sunk like rebar into the layer below.

Then there is the lie of abundance. "A slice of wedding cake is one inch wide and two inches deep," says the instruction sheet. No wonder the thing feeds eighty.

"What time will *you* be there?" Tina had said, and the question struck Rainey as oddly precise, as if Rainey's arrival from West Tenth Street was of more interest than the cake's.

Around two, Rainey said. The cake's coming at three. And Tina said, "I'll come around four," and Rainey had a thought so crazy it seemed almost sane: *She's going to see Howard when she knows I'll be out.* But that was ridiculous. All they had together were a few clarinet lessons and some staring contests.

While the baker's apprentice sets the three layers on the table, Rainey takes the slicing diagrams from Leah and studies them. They look like clocks.

"One *inch?*" says Leah. "Is this for real?" But the baker's apprentice isn't listening. He floats a circle of parchment onto the largest tier. Then he lifts tier 2 by its cardboard under-belly and deposits it on the parchment. The intercom buzzes. The baker's apprentice starts frosting the seams, squeezing ribbons of buttercream from a fabric sack.

Rainey lets Tina in. "Hey," says Tina. She has no trouble meeting Rainey's eyes. That's a good sign, right? Rainey sniffs. Tina smells faintly like sandalwood. She often does.

Stop it, thinks Rainey. Half the people you know smell like sandalwood.

Tina edges up to the table. She nods at Leah—no smile—and Rainey sees she is going to have to work at this, she is going to have to force this friendship. Tina sets an anatomy book unnervingly close to the cake. She never goes anywhere without a textbook; she'll study standing up in the subway. It drives Rainey crazy; she'd rather talk.

Tina watches the baker's apprentice squeezing out frosting and says, "Can I try?"

He ignores her. "Tina," says Leah. "Don't."

"I've got surgeon's hands," says Tina. "I'm not going to ruin your cake."

"She's not going to ruin your cake because she's not going to do it," says Rainey.

Man and buttercream remain in deep communion. Finally he says, "There's a bit of an art to it. If I wasn't free, they'd stake the cake and deliver it whole."

"'Stake the cake'?" says Leah.

"For stability," he says. "Sharpen a dowel and hammer it down the middle."

"Hah," says Tina. "Like killing a vampire."

The baker's apprentice blanches. "You haven't said you like it."

It's both effusive and restrained, this wedding cake, strewn with café-au-lait roses. Rainey still wishes she'd managed mice.

"I love it," says Leah. "You should sign it."

He looks around her bare-walled studio. "Where's your wedding?"

"She came to her senses," says Rainey lightly. "Where's your cloche?"

He touches his uncovered hair.

"Take it apart first," he says. "Eat from the bottom, not the top."

As soon as he leaves, Tina picks up the knife that Leah has set on the windowsill.

"Wait," says Rainey, touching her wrist.

She watches Leah circle the table, studying the three-story confection as if looking for an angle of attack. Saliva pools in the hollow of Rainey's tongue. The thing is flawless, extravagant. Maybe, for Leah, it's too perfect. Maybe she's afraid her appetites might tarnish it.

"Wait for what?" says Tina coolly. "This is the kind of thing I'm good at, remember?" She looks at Leah and sets the edge of the blade on the top tier.

Back off, thinks Rainey. You don't have anything to prove.

"Sugar causes adhesions," says Tina. "That's when tissue sticks to tissue. You're going to be a wreck."

HOW IT SAVED HER

Rainey enters the dark tidal pool between streetlights on a side street. He steps out of a doorway, grabs her jacket at the back of the neck, and twists.

"I have a knife," he says. Rainey feels a point of pressure above her hip and a prickle of sweat in the April night. "Wallet and rings. *That* ring."

He must be an actor, rehearsing, right? Her feet seem to lift from the sidewalk. Does everyone float when they're being mugged? She feels in her bag, finds her wallet, and reaches back with it. The wallet contains three dollars, a library card, tokens. But the diamond ring—that was her grandmother's. She considers the pressure of the knife through her denim jacket. It could be a pen.

"The ring's stuck," she says. This is theoretically true: it's barely come off since her mother put it there: not even when her father hoped to sell it.

The mugger jabs. It hurts. It could still be a pen. "Want me to cut it off?" he says.

From a great distance she hears herself say, *Yeah, I think you should slice my finger off, dumbfuck,* and then a man says, "Lucy?"

He comes out of nowhere from behind and circles around to face them. "Lucy, I thought it was you," he says. But they have never met. She makes out black-rimmed glasses, the kind of bland leather jacket worn by the good guys, an expression both cautious and expectant. "Is this a friend?"

Half behind her, the mugger drapes a proprietary arm around her shoulders and pokes her with the sharp object. So it would not be safe to say no. Instead, she makes a tiny, deliberate noise of distress. "I don't feel so good," she says. Then she collapses with some force to the sidewalk and grabs the stranger's white-socked ankle.

"Help me," she says, closing her eyes partway and twitching as she imagines epilepsy might look. "I'm having a seizure. Don't leave me." From the sidewalk she considers her mugger's chinos. Didn't men with knives wear jeans? So graceless to lie twitching on the ground, but she does, gripping the stranger's ankle and pleading, "Don't leave me, I'm having a seizure." She hears her mugger say, "I'll go for help." She feels a hand on her arm. She smells lemon verbena.

"Tell me you're faking."

She opens one eye fully. Jerks her right leg just in case.

"He's gone." The man extends a hand. He wears a school ring. Who loves school that much? "You had to be faking— no one talks in a seizure," he says.

She pulls herself up by his hand and stands, trembling in every limb though she tries to stop. "He wanted to saw my finger off."

"I knew something was wrong," the man says. "The way he was standing behind you, and you handing him something. Are you okay?" She is not okay; her wrists and knees feel like they're vibrating. "I'm not done rescuing you," he says. "You get another wish."

She touches his hand, lightly. "Who *are* you? My guardian angel?" She likes having to stretch to kiss him on the cheek. The lemon verbena must be his soap.

"Yes," he says. "I'm Clayton, and you are my goddess."

She flinches. "I'm a starving artist," she says. "If you're granting wishes, I'll take a cheap apartment." She laughs, though she is shaking worse. She has had it with Damien and Gordy and Radmila worshipping her father and living in *her house*, though she'll never leave. "Actually," she says, "just walk me to the subway and give me a token."

"Actually," he says.

She needs him to put his arm around her, and suddenly he does. They walk slowly toward the neon promise of a Broadway RESTAURANT sign. "Actually what?"

"My brother-in-law manages rent-controlled apartments. You could look at a studio tomorrow."

She leans into this man. She considers his ankle, how it saved her, how it looked both sturdy and wrong in its scruffy white sock, as if he were receiving flawed signals about how to be in the world and did not care. It makes her feel tender, this ankle. It makes her feel safe.

"Actually," she says, "I'm okay where I am," but she lays her head on his shoulder as he signals for a cab.

SHE WONDERS IF THE birds can smell orchids and bromeliads from the wholesaler downstairs, and if it reminds them of some distant home. The birds are African gray parrots Clayton breeds in his loft. They are the hue of expensive menswear, with a shot of red at the tail like a bright tie, and they climb up and down the outsides of their cages muttering to themselves. One periodically bursts into the ring of a telephone.

A powdery dust sifts from under the birds' wings; it shortens Rainey's breath. Clayton mists them with a plant sprayer, but it barely helps.

He lives in the loft, though it isn't legal. He makes his own pasta and chocolate truffles in the makeshift kitchen and deals coke from a locked metal cabinet. Rainey wonders how the parrots feel about this life—the cooking smells, especially when small fowl are involved; the coke dust she imagines must hang in the air; the clipped wings.

A few weeks after the mugging Clayton serves her quail wrapped in bacon. The quail are not much bigger than her fists. A parrot could grip one in a chalky claw. Rainey thinks she might faint with pleasure at the stuffing. She has stopped seeing friends, even Tina or Leah; when she isn't working on a tapestry in her pink room, she's at the loft, wheezing, chirring at the birds. She goes home, though, every night: a cat returning to its lair.

They eat in silence. Clayton serves sautéed spinach and roasted carrots. "I had to isolate three birds today," he finally says. "They started feather plucking. They look half naked. It's so sad." He names a disease that sounds to Rainey like *citizen*. Citizen feather-and-death disease? Citizen hoof-and-mouth disease? "Or they could just be miserable about something," he says.

Yeah, she thinks, like smelling quail in the oven. She lifts a miniature drumstick, and meat drops from the bone; she catches it with her tongue. "God, you're amazing."

"You're right," says Clayton. "I am amazing. It could be the foie gras in the stuffing, though." He leans forward. "Move in with me."

But then she'd be like one of the birds. She wants him to desire her, and she wants him to slink away. She gives him a long, sorrowful look.

He reaches for his wine and pushes his chair back. Rainey feels the thrill of something imminent, the air electrically charged. He stands and moves in to kiss her, still holding his wineglass. She pulls away. Clayton sighs. A sprig of dark hair flops over his forehead.

"Would it help to know that I'm working on a parrot surprise for you?" Clayton looks right at her. Most men look at her chest.

"It sounds like dinner. Parrot Surprise." Sometimes when Rainey is in Clayton's loft, she feels like nibbling her own feathers out.

"I'm teaching Perdita to say 'Come live with me and be my love.'"

"I have a home, Clayton."

"It's from the sonnet," he says. "'And we will all the pleasures prove.'"

Her father quotes Shakespeare at her, too. She has waited for Howard to notice the hours she spends at Clayton's loft, but lately he's been gone by the time she wakes, spending days in some recording studio instead of sleeping. Ridiculously, she stumbles down in her nightgown some mornings and looks for a note. Howard's attention is like the sun. Too much burns the edges of her leaves, yet the atmosphere is thin without it.

Clayton smooths her long hair behind her ear and touches her cheekbone. He puts his free hand on her breast and leaves it. She smells lemon verbena. She likes it.

"And he can cook, too," says Clayton.

"If you're waiting for me to say yes," says Rainey, more drily than she intends, "stop." She means: Stop asking,

because I'm not moving in. She means: Stop being a gentleman and for Chrissake ravish me.

But she realizes, as he pulls away, that all he registers is
stop. It's a big misunderstanding. It makes Rainey itch. She
wonders if he was ever wild enough for that intense ex-wife
of his. "Okay," says Clayton. He takes his seat and goes to
work on another quail. "You win, Rainey. Go figure out what
you want."

She takes an enormous swallow of wine. "Wait," she says,
but he shakes his head.

He'll forgive her. Right? He's her guardian angel. And he
can cook, too.

She blurts the first lie she can think of and is shocked to
feel it expand in her heart, spreading wings, becoming truth.
"I can't move in," she says. "My father needs me."

FLY OR DIE

Order to self: Go to a normal party and be normal about it. Leave in thirty minutes. *Go.*

The bird-boyfriend's party hemorrhages music. It's in the Flower District, all dirty-windowed lofts. Leah feels an internal coiling—that's twenty-three feet of small intestine, telling her to go home.

Stupid girl. She will look stupid; she will say stupid things. But she only has to look stupid till she finds Rainey or the boyfriend.

Up five flights, joins a semisolid volume of humans. Whirling molecules, all of them, wedging through a doorway into the bird-boyfriend's enormous loft. Grace Slick sings in a slow, throbbing Spanish. *Para escapar*, Leah hears—*to escape.*

Loft is packed. From the hall she sees people inside dancing to Grace. Young man tacks ahead of her, pocking the air with invisible drumsticks and jostling her into the wall. His movement opens a slender channel. She steps into it and is subsumed. Where are the bird-boyfriend's parrots? Stashed in bedroom? Impossible to spot Rainey or the boyfriend, Clayton, or Tina Dial. Needing purpose, Leah squeezes upstream and locates the rum punch. There's no ladle, just take a baby Dixie and dunk.

She dips and drinks, and drinks again. Libations flow straight through the blood-brain barrier. Lacing self through crowd, she tries to keep the third punch from sloshing. Cigarettes bob and jab in inattentive hands. Reaches a wall, finally. Plasters self to it. Posture is her cloak. *My friend just went for drinks*, her eyes say. *Why don't you drop dead?*

Miss L looks hot, though. Leah admits it. Strappy pink leotard, deliberate clash with red hair. Black Genny skirt, fifteen amazing dollars in the Irvington thrift shop. Also men's black Tony Lama boots, size eight and a half. They cost even less than the skirt. When she wears them to work, they collect a dun-colored dust from the ankles down— particulate traces of Purina mouse chow, which she parcels out in the lab.

Notice me, she thinks. *Stay away.*

Someone changes the record, and Jefferson Airplane comes on loud: rabbits, dormice, pills. Now Leah sees them, deep in the crowd. *Together*, they are dancing *together*, Rainey, Tina, Clayton. Leah, riveted, can't tell who is the third, the odd one out.

What would happen if she squeezed through the crowd and tried to become the fourth? Rainey would turn to dance with Clayton. That would leave Tina, who should first do no harm. But Tina would turn away.

Then Leah would be dancing alone. So forget it.

She manages a good five minutes this way, partying by proxy, when a woman comes and stands nearby.

Her body language is far more fluent than Leah's. *I've never been nervous a moment in my life.* Her hair is a fountain of ringlets, and her feet are bare, in red stilettos.

Leah looks at her from the white of her eye, and the woman turns to her.

"There is a smaller party," she says, "in the last room down the hall." Then she pushes off from the wall.

Leah knows a rabbit hole when she sees one.

Touch base, says her brain. But she pushes off, too, and heads for the hall. Passes the bathroom, so noted by the line, and comes to the final door, posted with a sign that reads OFF LIMITS.

Surely not to Those Who Are Following a Sylph?

The bedroom is empty of people, crowded at the far end with large, covered birdcages on wheeled stands. The birds under their cloths are silent. Stunned by darkness or rock and roll? A high, open window gapes onto the night.

No sylph. Either she has chosen the wrong room or the wrong party, where she has made the narcissistic, puppyish mistake of following a woman with a Laeliocattleya mouth.

Outside the open window, a match ignites. The woman is floating out there in the night. No: she is sitting on the fire-escape stairs. "What took you so long?" she says.

She probably got out there with a neat little hop. Leah folds herself through and squats, facing her, trembling, fishing for a cigarette. "I'm Leah."

The woman reaches out. Leah's right hand obediently goes to hers. Instead of shaking it the woman turns it over, examines the small print on her palm.

"I'm a skeptic," says Leah, and pulls it back.

"Most intelligent people are," says the woman. She reaches for Leah's hand again. "May I? You have a powerful head line. Deeply incised." She looks up. "It correlates nicely to the phalange of logic." She strokes the base of Leah's thumb. "You do your own taxes. Numbers don't intimidate."

"Ha," says Leah, trying to be neutral. She pulls her hand back again, but the woman holds it firm.

"Your heart line is less pronounced," she says. "Put it this way. Your head line is a river. Your heart line is a drip from the kitchen faucet."

This woman has looked in Leah's mirror. She has seen the flaw. "Remind me to call the super," says Leah, and then, "Oh, shit," because how will she find Rainey in an off-limits room?

The woman looks up as if Leah has finally revealed something of interest. "Someone needs to teach you how to have fun," she says, and drops Leah's hand.

Leah jams the hand in her jacket pocket. "I should go in. Have some fun," she adds.

The woman stands, nearly losing a heel to the gaps in the fire escape. "Maybe it's not your kind of party. There's a secret way out." The alley, five stories below, is an abyss with trash cans. "Not down," says the woman. "Up."

One flight to the roof. The woman removes her right shoe, kisses it, and throws. It sails over the parapet. She hands Leah the other shoe. "Here," she says. "Throw."

"I can't." The shoe seems to pulse in her hand like a heart. Leah backs away. "I'm meeting someone. You want me to go fetch that?" *Fetch*. Like a puppy.

"Someone?" says the woman musically.

"It's her party," says Leah. "I mean it's her boyfriend's loft—"

"Spare me," says the woman, "I was married to the boyfriend."

Across the lit room, the door opens. Rainey peers in. "Leah?"

Leah cups her cigarette and freezes. Rainey sniffs. She smells their smoke, Leah thinks. "Hey," she says. It comes out half croak. "Out here."

"Levinson, I've been looking for you for an *hour*." Rainey sticks her head out the open window. "Zola," she says.

Zola exhales a rope of smoke toward Rainey while Leah falls in love with her name.

"I was looking for you for an hour, too," says Leah. "I got claustrophobic."

"Hello, Rainey." Zola laughs, a raspy, private sort of chuckle.

"You guys *know* each other?" says Rainey.

"We just met," says Leah.

"We're old friends," says Zola. "We were just leaving." A sash of her smoke dissolves between them.

Rainey looks at Leah hard. "We're not going anywhere," Leah says.

"If you leave with her," says Rainey, "you're going somewhere."

Leah would like to go somewhere, actually. She would go somewhere with Rainey—but Rainey has sealed herself unto Tina Dial since something like sixth grade. Tina shadows Rainey like a twin, and Leah wants to taste that kind of dangerous alliance, something deeper even than friendship, a collusion that sucks up the oxygen in its sphere and thrives on tiny cruelties.

Zola looks at the two women. "Leah, darlin', is there glue on that shoe?"

Leah kisses the shoe quickly and hurls it. Rainey says, "Big mistake," but Leah gives her what she hopes is a mysterious smile and turns away. Zola starts up the ladder. Her bare feet flash on the dark rungs. Leah follows her to the roof. Zola waits barefoot at the top while Leah crunches across the tar paper and trots back wearing a shoe on each hand, flapping them in triumph.

In the stairwell they shoulder into a chain of people,

thread their way outside, meet up in the silvery bath of a streetlight.

"Well," says Leah, fear setting in. "That was fun."

"Climbing a fire escape? That's not fun, my heart," says Zola. "Spending my alimony, that would be fun. Champagne at the Brasserie, that would be fun."

Leah can't talk.

"I think we must get you a cab," says Zola. She looks down the empty block. "Let's try Eighth," she says. Then, her voice low: "Drop me?"

Not a normal person, warns Leah's brain. Her heart bangs against the bars, the molecules flying apart. Mysterious stranger might move in too close, breathe her air. Leah is a person who requires much space, even in her fantasy life.

But she wraps arms around self in lucky leather jacket and murmurs: "Drop you where?"

RAINEY TELEPHONES EVERY FOUR or five days. Leah is never free.

"I'm gonna sic Tina on you," says Rainey. "You used to be almost fun. What's happening?"

"I'm just busy." Leah lowers her voice. She's in the lab office, where she has no privacy and is not supposed to take personal calls. She works, when she is not handling mice, under a greenish bank of lights. The lab manager, Lawrence, makes notes in a data book; the other lab tech, Marina, waters leggy plants. "Work is happening," says Leah.

"Maybe Zola's happening."

Leah blushes so hard she is sure Rainey can hear her capillaries expand over the phone. Her brain starts mocking her. *Naïveté's happening. Proclivities are happening.* How does Rainey sense these things? But maybe Leah can sense things, too. Maybe Rainey never noticed, in high school, the current between Tina and Howard flowing so strong it electrified the follicles of Leah's hair.

"I'm running an experiment," she says. Lawrence looks up from the data book and starts to talk. She makes wild arm movements in his direction.

"Don't tell me," says Rainey. "You're studying what happens when you put crazy lying ex-wives together with tall sexy lab technicians who don't know remotely what they've gotten into."

"I have no idea what you're talking about," says Leah.

OH, FUCK. YOU KNOW why Zola lied? Leah wouldn't have come, that's why. She has rat duty in the morning, and when Zola steps out of their taxi on Tenth Avenue, Leah can see they're not at a nightclub. Meaning it's not like Area or wherever people go.

And Zola—impatiently tapping her foot on the sidewalk, which is sort of her way of laughing—Zola is not a hostess.

For evidence Leah has the orange-neon silhouette glowing in the window—a homunculus of hair, bosom, and flank, burning against black glass. Then there's the name, Treasure Chest, and the truck-rumbled neighborhood, not the best.

"I don't think so," she says, and steps back off the curb. But their cab has pulled away.

Zola tugs her, in pulses, back onto the sidewalk. "Ten minutes," she says.

Leah's silent. It's less entangling than *yes*.

Zola says, "There are two little things you have to get straight." Leah shakes her head. "Your drink," says Zola, "and your cover story."

Hail another fucking cab, says the cerebral cortex. But somewhere around the brain stem Leah's also thinking: Move and she drops your hand, is that what you want?

"Tonight," says Zola, "you order Jack and ginger. Or Jack and Coke."

"Why?"

"Because all the girls do," says Zola, "and trust me, in this business, you don't want to stand out."

"I'm not in this business."

"If a customer talks to you, be sweet."

"No customers," says Leah.

Zola swings Leah's hand like a child. "If he asks why you're there, say something mindless. Say you're writing an article on exotic dancers, if it makes you happy."

"For what magazine?"

Zola snorts. "He doesn't care what magazine. He's going

to say, Really? You a writer? Or Really? You a Virgo? Say yes. Be nice."

"I'm not going in," says Leah. "There are naked people in there."

"Not really," says Zola. "The men have to keep their clothes on."

"I can't."

Oh, and her name—

Her name, Zola says, is Lacey. An alliterative to Leah. An easy, cheerleader Lacey. All blonde hair and boyfriends. Lacey Chase, two words that slide on the same string easy as pearls.

But Zola is just Zola.

"I gave up my last name when I was fourteen," she says. "You won't find a trace of me anywhere."

"FREDDIE, I'D LIKE YOU to meet my girlfriend, Lacey."

Is that *girlfriend* as in *girl friend*, or *girlfriend* as in *girlfriend*? Leah's brain starts chewing on it: one word or two? Then it stops, distracted by the slightly seductive note—deferential, with a twist of helpless—Zola's taking with this Freddie.

The man turns on his barstool and inspects them. His eyebrows step down toward the bridge of his nose, and his hair is pulled into a ponytail. He wears a black jacket over a navy T-shirt. Leah hates that, black with navy. It took her all of college to get used to black with brown.

She spends about two seconds on Freddie, however,

because a woman is doing something fluid on a stage behind him. The woman wears shiny black panties that lace at the crotch, and something papery bristles out of her waistband. A misnomer, waistband—this garment stops way south of her navel. Leah stares a little harder, realizes she's looking at money. Bills, folded and refolded lengthwise, inserted under the elastic at the hip.

Also, she has no top on, which Leah finds mesmerizing, and one breast is larger than the other, which she finds revelatory. Why isn't this a disqualifying flaw?

"Your girlfriend Lacey," Freddie repeats, and Leah realizes he's watching her watch the dancer. She looks back at him with alarm.

"Mm-hmm," says Zola musically, "the one I told you about." Told him about? "We're going downstairs now, okay?"

A thought floats into Leah's brain: *She's afraid of him.*

"You do that," says Freddie. "See you real soon, Lace."

Zola leads her past the stage and through a curtain of plastic beads, clicky and clear like drugstore diamonds, and down a flight of stairs. Under bare bulbs, Leah watches their shadows spill ahead of them, then slink around behind. She follows Zola into a basement bathroom marked ADIES.

"Congratulations," says Zola.

"On what?" Strange, why a toilet area so obviously crawling with microbes would also be brilliantly lit.

"You passed."

"Passed what?" Leah is thinking she means some kind of girlfriend test, the way Leah looked at that dancer.

"Your audition," says Zola. "You can take your clothes off anytime now."

It turns out there's a biological basis for those cartoons where a person's eyeballs pop out. Leah feels air cooling her eye sockets. "You lied to me," she says. Her red hair blares at her from the mirror. "Ten minutes are up." Though she would like to stop and watch the dancer for a minute on her way out. Maybe two minutes, if no one notices. She could stand far away, near the door. "I can't do this," she says. "I can't do any single part of this."

Zola upends her makeup bag into the sink—big clatter of Maybelline, tweezers, loose change. "I didn't lie." On tiptoe, she nudges a dark line along the rim of an eyelid with a short pencil. "I said I was taking you to work."

Leah marvels at the ice forming deep in her fingers— classic fight-or-flight.

"You're out of your mind," she says. *Fly or die.*

Zola taps a sign by the towel dispenser. It's lettered in careful capitals and cheaply framed, like an old diploma.

"Homework," says Zola. "Read. There will be a quiz."

HOUSE RULES

DANCERS IF YOU ARE LATE FOR YOUR SET YOU WILL BE FINED $5 "PER MINUTE"

ANY DANCER LATE 3X IS "OUT"

TIPS ON STAGE ONLY. ANY DANCER WHO ACCEPTS
TIPS "ON THE FLOOR" WILL BE FINED $25

DANCERS MUST WEAR PANTY HOSE

ANY QUESTIONS SEE MGMT.

"No," says Leah. Though she finds the sign, all regimental with rules, curiously calming. The sign implies a structure to things where she had presumed chaos.

Bare bulbs light up Zola's hair, ringlets both flawlessly turned and wild. "You think I'm not serious." She puts down a compact, rummages in her tote, and hands Leah a balled-up pair of panty hose. Sheer. Sandalfoot. Size D, the tallest. Leah's size, in fact. Leah is what people like to call a tall glass of water, and sometimes she thinks she is about as interesting.

Where is a good, shapeless lab coat when she really needs one?

"No," says Leah, and starts laughing. Somewhere deep inside, a brake slips. "No," she says. Even without the laugh, it sounds slightly hysterical, this *no*. It almost sounds like *yes*, this *no*. "This is crazy," she says. Thinking: *My* breasts are the same size. I am a symmetrical person having an asymmetrical crisis.

Commandeer the sole toilet stall; slide the bolt. Tap the door. *Base.*

The stall is sordid at a cellular level, with amoeba-shaped overlays of dirt on the tile. An old toothbrush would be nice, and some Clorox, because she can tell no one has ever scrubbed this grout. It's a nasty microbial crust, this grout. Bacteria are probably in the throes of cell division all over this grout.

She studies the graffiti, hoping for some perspective, and encounters several permutations of FREDDIE IS A SHIT.

And she was wrong about something else, too: the law of gravity does not apply down here in Basement World. Indeed, the floor has already let go of her feet, and she is fully three feet off the ground, consequence of forgetting to breathe, when the bathroom door wheezes open. Fingernails click on the door of her stall.

"Hellooo? This is not funny, honey. I'm desperate."

Leah peers at Desperate's feet under the door. Black toe-nails—painted, not bruised. A high arch. Personally she'd use pumice around the heels, but with those shoes—spiky, strappy—no one's going to inspect.

"Zola," says Desperate, "could you explain to your friend? I can't afford another ten-dollar pee."

Jesus, how many people were expecting her tonight?

Zola says calmly, "Lacey? Are you listening? You can go in the sink for all I care, but you have to get out fifteen seconds ago."

"I can't," says Leah, but she concedes the stall, still holding the balled-up panty hose. Desperate shoves past her, a discordant blur of peach satin and blue-black hair, and Zola, still engaged with the mirror, thrusts a lipstick in Leah's direction. Makeup—that's why they burn so much wattage down here.

"What's a ten-dollar pee?"

It's a new lipstick Zola hands her, color like blackberry stain, tip sharp as a knife. Then she touches the back of Leah's hand, whispers. In the mirror, Leah sees her lips move. In her hair, Leah feels her breath. What gets lost are the words. And as it turns out, she cannot lip-read from memory.

You are beautiful.

No.

Do this one thing for me.

No.

Don't you know where you are, my heart? This is the brink.

No.

Just open your arms and fall. Fly or die.

Zola's back at her makeup. And Leah can't ask. But here is one thing she can do. She can commune with this vampire lipstick. She can incise a blood-black heart along her upper lip.

No hour with Rainey has felt this dangerous, this close.

Desperate barges out of the stall, says, "God, I never learn," jockeys for a sliver of mirror, pursues something in her teeth, then flings the door open, talking straight through. "You're Zola's friend, right? You're the virgin, right? You need a Tums? Listen," she adds, as the door severs their connection, "you'll be great."

"No," says Leah.

"Delilah," says Zola, like that explains everything.

"What's a ten-dollar pee?"

Zola turns to her again, takes Leah's chin in one hand, wields a pencil. Midnight blue.

"You're better than many," says Zola, drawing a curve along Leah's eyelashes, then smudging it with a pinkie. "Didn't throw up. Didn't back out."

"No," says Leah, "this is not happening," and curls her toes around the edge of the cliff.

Her mother said, I've had it with detangling this hair. Rainey, sit still. Gordy, you try it. Start at the bottom and comb.

Her mother said, Will you look at this drawing, Howard? Who draws an antelope in *kindergarten*? Will you stop playing for one minute and look?

Her mother said, You just got yourself a job, Gordy. She sits so still when you do it. Look, she doesn't *breathe*.

Her mother said, The problem with a pet is you are tied to it forever, so no.

Her mother said, When you sew a dart, leave a tail of thread and tie it in a knot.

Her mother said, Your father is the most charismatic man I've ever known. There is nothing he could ask me that I wouldn't do.

Her mother said, That's a sleepover, baby. When I go into

Gordy's room? Mommies can have sleepovers. So can Daddies. It's not just little girls.

Her mother said, Every morning I go up on the roof at six o'clock and pray for twenty minutes. It keeps me from coming apart. Her mother said, Coming apart, coming apart—it's just a crazy thing I feel.

Her mother said, Every woman needs a signature, and mine is tea-rose oil. You don't need to hear this when you're eight, do you? But you need to make your mark as a woman. You might as well think about it now.

Her mother said, We're having one of those grown-up parties, baby—close your door tonight and stay in your room.

Her mother said, Rainey Royal, you baste like a dream. That is the neatest hem in New York.

Her mother said, It's like having two husbands, I swear to God, except neither of them provides.

Her mother said, If you don't like what goes on in this house, Rainey, don't be a part of it. (Her mother did not say what to do if it was already a part of her.)

Her mother said, You can keep your groupies, Howard. You can keep your loverboy Gordy—that is one sick friendship. I want something real in my life.

Her mother said, Sometimes I go sit by the washing machine, Howard, just to escape the fucking jazz. I don't care how good it is.

Her mother said, Rainey, sometimes a woman has to do something for herself.

Her mother said, Say something.

Her mother said, I'll write, I promise.

Her mother said, Maybe in a few years you can live with me.

Her mother said, We'll see.

TINA'S GRANDMOTHER DIES, AND Rainey stays four days on East 101st Street. She sleeps in Señora Colón's narrow bed and folds the dead woman's enormous clothes. She makes Tina eat. She follows Tina slowly up the aisle of a packed church and watches, shocked, as Tina presses her lips to the dead woman's forehead. *Cath, give me strength*, she prays, and bends to kiss what feels exactly like the old, veined marble of Lala's kitchen counters. *Thank you*, Tina whispers. She has barely spoken in days.

Rainey comes home to a front hall footprinted with dry mud that no one has mopped.

"A pipe broke downstairs," Rainey's father says from the piano. "We got the plumber out of bed."

Rainey runs down to the basement utility room. It's empty now, swamped with two inches of water that flow out to form a delta of muck.

She stalks back into the parlor. "Where's my stuff?"

"I'm composing." Howard teases out a flutter of high notes.

"Where are my boxes from the utility room?"

"*Your* boxes? It looked like trash." Howard stops playing, tries a short variation, stops again. "Everything got soaked. I threw it out. Tax records, too. We better not get audited."

"It looked like *trash*? My mother's clothing looked like *trash*?" Rainey can catalog every piece. She packed it away when she was thirteen, when Linda left: a Marimekko miniskirt, an Indian-print jumper, a wardrobe Linda stitched herself on a secondhand Singer before it died.

Howard sets his palms on his thighs, turns to Rainey, and says, as if explaining simple arithmetic for the third time, "It should have been thrown out years ago. When she took off, if you ask me."

"I had photo albums in there." Rainey wraps a long hank of hair around her finger, pulls it taut, and fights the temptation to chew on it. "I had her bangle bracelets."

"You could have told me, Daughter," says Howard. "I opened the boxes and saw wet clothes."

"I don't care if they're soaked." The hair sneaks into Rainey's mouth. "I'm bringing them back in."

But now she can't recall if she saw boxes at the curb when she came home. She can't remember if any townhouse on the block still had trash on the street. Maybe garbage trucks came while she was comforting Tina and inhaling Tina's boyfriend, Eric. Eric is a tattoo artist who etches scenes of old New York—ships, buildings, even battles—down people's arms and backs. The rules say she cannot steal Eric. The rules do not say anything about standing very still, one inch too close, admiring the golden hairs on the arm that guides the needle.

"I'm sorry, babe. You should have written on the cartons."

Rainey dips her head back to look at the ceiling cherubs.

"I can't move," she says, and this is true. She is scoured out.

Howard snaps his fingers twice. Rainey still stands with her head tipped back.

"Look, if it's such a big deal," says Howard, "your aunt Laurette's a clutter hound."

Rainey sees Laurette about once a year, maybe twice—lunch, it's always lunch, and it's always at Tom's, never at home; and it's got to be a tuna-fish sandwich; the rest of the menu might as well be toxic. Howard might mock her for going, but Rainey likes to hear Laurette talk: her aunt has her mother's voice.

"I see Laurette sometimes," she says cautiously. The clutter-hound thing is news to her.

"Then you know," says Howard. "She's kind of a shut-in. A little nuts. But she might have things that belonged to Linda."

"How do I know you're not with the landlord?"

"'Cause you know me, Laurette." Rainey traces with a finger the marker scars on the lobby wall and leans into the intercom. "Please, I just want to talk to you about my mom."

"I can't know who you are."

"Come down and look."

"My niece doesn't come to my apartment. No one comes to my apartment."

"Laurette, just come down and *see*."

"Wait there," says Laurette.

Rainey has time to finish her cigarette before Laurette descends the lobby stairs in flip-flops and comes to the glass front door. Her thick, crinkly hair is unbound, and three silver rings flash from one hand as she lets Rainey in. "You're not supposed to come here," she says, stepping back.

"Don't be mad." Rainey follows her into the lobby. Instead of pressing the elevator button, though, Laurette sits on the steps. Rainey leans against the mailboxes and twirls her hair, hoping she looks endearing. She has no idea what the problem is. "Can't we go upstairs?"

"No," says Laurette. "We cannot. How is your mother?"

Rainey is suddenly aware of the air in her sinuses. She wonders if her face looks stuck. She has no idea how her mother is. Linda Royal lives on an ashram in Boulder, or maybe it is some kind of cult. Rainey is twenty-two, and for nine years the ashram has been Linda's family.

"She's great," she says. "We still talk twice a week. Listen." She slips into her best little-girl voice and tucks her head into her shoulder. "I have to ask you about her, but I can't do it in the lobby."

"Try," says Laurette in an encouraging way. "I can't have guests."

"Why? Why can't you?"

Laurette laughs. "Oh, Niece."

Rainey feels herself deflected in that same way as when her father calls her Daughter. "I don't get it. *Why* must we always meet at Tom's?"

"Because it's right on the corner. And my place is a mess."

You're an artist, Rainey wants to say, *you're allowed to live in a mess*. And it is true that Laurette is a painter, though she talks about it like a past life, and Rainey has never seen her work.

In high school, in the third-floor girls' room, Rainey made Mary Gage eat half a cigarette. She made Anita Levy cut off her own braid, and she made Leah stick her tongue out for a square of paper that Leah believed was acid. The important things were out of her control, but sometimes she could make people do stuff by using a voice that sounded like melting sugar, and she summons now her best bullying voice for Laurette.

"Well, guess what." She walks to the stairs and puts a foot on the second step, so that her leg is between Laurette's knees. She looks down at her aunt and smiles. "You're having company now. I don't care if it's a mess."

To her surprise, Laurette meets her gaze without blinking. After a moment Laurette pulls herself up by the banister and stands, so that Rainey has to look up at her. "Don't you dare try to intimidate me," says Laurette.

Behind Rainey, a door clicks open and squeals. Laurette looks toward the sound.

"Shit." She lunges up the stairs two at a time.

Rainey, following her, glances back. In the lobby a man with a wide broom stands in an apartment doorway. "*You* talk to her," he calls. "She hasn't brought a damn thing to the basement yet."

She turns and runs after her aunt, hears the *thunk, thunk, thunk* of deadbolts turning and corners Laurette at a third-floor apartment door. The door swings open and thuds on some obstruction. Laurette squeezes quickly into a long hall with ornate crown moldings. She blocks the doorway and peers at Rainey.

"That was the super," she whispers. "Now go."

Impossible. Traces of her mother must lie in this place. Rainey jams her foot between the casement and the door. She watches Laurette tip her head toward the stairs, listening. "He could come up," says Rainey casually. "You might need me."

Laurette looks down at Rainey's sneaker. "All right, all right," she hisses. "Get *in*."

Inside, as Laurette leans past her to lock the deadbolts, Rainey examines with a thrill what blocked the door. Along the length of the hallway is a fortress wall of stacked magazines, newspapers, and cardboard boxes, two piles deep and high as her waist. It allows only a narrow trail for walking.

"Don't look," says Laurette. "It's terrible. I don't want anybody looking."

Two gray cats patrol the top of the magazine wall. Rainey strokes one as she follows her aunt. She smells mildewed paper. She brushes against newspaper edges that look like shredded lace and imagines the air filled with infinitesimal paper particles, yellowed and flammable. If she lit a cigarette, the place might ignite. Halfway down they pass the kitchen, where the refrigerator is consumed almost to the freezer by shopping bags and leaning, unframed canvases.

She's the artist in the family, Linda used to say, as if there were room for only one. But Linda could copy a dress in a magazine, just by eye.

"My coffeemaker's broken," says Laurette, her voice catching.

It isn't broken, it's buried, thinks Rainey. A pigeon flutters past the kitchen window, which overlooks an air shaft. Rainey, trapped by trash, feels herself grounded, caged.

Laurette hugs herself as she walks. "We'll talk in the living room. Then I'll take you to lunch."

Rainey remembers that voice, her mother's voice, singing her to sleep. "That's cool," she says.

The living room is packed with layers of detritus almost to her thigh, like the strata of unearthed civilizations. Trailing from the mouths of shopping bags and strewn on boxes are objects so varied they make Rainey feel faint: sweaters, books, an antler, a guitar with no strings, two wooden-backed oval hairbrushes, a red ring box. A marble mantel juts up above it all. Set nearby are two shapely pink armchairs and a sofa in yellow damask. The trail ends at a closed door that must lead to the bedroom.

"Move the magazines," says Laurette. She follows a trail to one chair, and gestures to the other.

Rainey's movements feel heavy, as if her legs must pull through river sludge. She wants to race down to the street and breathe. She relocates a stack of slick, heavy *National Geographics* from the seat cushion; they leave an oblong depression, where she sits. Sunlight, struggling through dirty windows, raises a nap of dust on the cardboard boxes.

I have every right to be here, she thinks. Old photos, paper dolls, report cards, anything Laurette may have salvaged from their girlhoods—such things would, in all fairness, be Rainey's, right? She imagines cutting these things up to make the largest and most beautiful paper tapestry of her life. She would call it, simply, *Linda*.

It would never be for sale.

Laurette leans toward Rainey. "I'm in a legal battle," she says. "It takes all my attention. You can't stay long."

It's true, Rainey can't stay all day. She's meeting Tina and Eric, and Tina is cooking. She's kept Señora Colón's apartment, but Rainey's moving her into the townhouse, rent-free: ally, sister, friend. Leah is busy tonight, or maybe not; Tina agitates her. Rainey plans to ask Eric for a sparrow at the top of her right breast. She is not sure Eric will agree to a sparrow, though. She is not sure Tina will agree to a breast. She *is* sure her father finds Eric ludicrous: "Tattoo *artist*? Is that a little inflated, babe?"

Yet Rainey likes sitting in the home of an actual aunt—a woman who once shared a bedroom with her mother. She likes being near these quirky objects—a beaded sweater, a blue vase shaped like a hand—that her mother may have touched. She might keep visiting Laurette just to sit in her pink chair like a niece and sip coffee from the excavated coffeemaker, and they will sift through ring boxes and old letters like a family.

"They want to evict me," says Laurette, patting a sprawling pile of mail in the shape of a coffee table. "They're blood-suckers. I'm no fire hazard. I don't even cook. I'm rent controlled—they want the apartment."

Rainey looks over the kindling that is Laurette's living room. "Can they do it?"

"Landlord's coming in a week to see if I got rid of my things. I'd like to see him throw out *his* things."

"I hear you," says Rainey automatically. She will do nothing but agree with her aunt.

"No, you don't." Laurette's eyes are rimmed with pink. Maybe it's the dust, Rainey thinks; her own eyes are begin-ning to itch. "I have every issue of Andy Warhol's *Interview* ever printed. I have *Art in America* going back to 1948, when my son was born. I have a *painting* in one of those magazines. I need to find it."

"You still paint?" It seems impossible: no space. On the walls are portraits of a boy and a young man done in pear-colored light. "That's Francis, right?" She remembers a young cousin who came over on long-ago holidays, who built houses out of chairs and sheets.

"I painted when I had a larger apartment. When I had a husband who brought his friends home for drinks, and a little boy who didn't think I was crazy." Laurette's eyes glitter. "Don't look, okay? Ask me about Linda. Then we'll go to Tom's. I don't go anywhere but Tom's. I'll buy you a tuna-fish sandwich."

"Or a grilled cheese."

"No," says Laurette.

Rainey nods. She will eat what Laurette tells her to eat.

"That ring," says Laurette, leaning forward to study Rainey's hand. "That was our mother's."

Rainey gets prickles on her arms. Is there going to be a fight about the ring? "Linda gave it to me," she says, and closes her other hand over the diamond bedded in rubies. *I can't take worldly goods where I'm going,* Linda Royal had said, and it had sounded then like her mother was going to die. Rainey's seen her mother twice in a decade. What is there to say about a ring, anyway?

"I wanted that ring," says Laurette. "But I got the silver," and Rainey thinks: *Must find silver.*

"Laurette," she says, "We had a flood. I lost everything of Linda's. Everything I'd saved. I thought you could give me something that belonged to her. Maybe some photos, too."

Laurette tilts her head and eyes Rainey warily as a crow. "You want some of my things?"

"Not yours." Rainey looks around the jumble of cartons and bags and says carefully, "Just a few of Linda's things. If you have them."

"You didn't come to talk," says Laurette. "You're one of the Dumpster people. You want to paw through everything and throw stuff out. You know what's in these boxes? The cross my mother wore. Birth certificates. Old photographs. Letters.

The silver. My mother's wedding china. I'm not opening one box, I'm not giving things away, and nothing goes in the trash."

At the thought of finding pieces of Linda in Laurette's junk, Rainey feels socked into her chair. Her left leg is wedged against a shopping bag that bulges with cooking pots and naked dolls. She wonders if Eric will have to rest his hand on her breast while he works.

"I think you should go."

"Listen," says Rainey. "I am not one of the Dumpster people. I am—I am a genius. I have a thought. We go through the cartons and save whatever's valuable. Then we store that someplace else. So if you get evicted, you'll always have it."

Laurette's eyes widen. Then she shakes her head. "I'm fighting this," she says. "Nothing leaves."

"They send a sheriff," says Rainey, though she is not sure sheriffs exist in New York City. "It's really bad. They carry your stuff down to the sidewalk." Laurette releases the chair and grips her head. "They drop it at the curb," says Rainey. "You can't guard everything. People pick it up and walk away with it."

"This is untenable," says Laurette.

"Then the garbage trucks come," says Rainey, thinking, *And I ought to know.* She listens without mercy to Laurette's jagged breaths. Her own secret stash had been neat, organized, hidden. Things Left Behind by Linda Royal.

"If you don't go through the boxes," says Rainey, drumming on one with her fingertips, "those trucks could be carting away the wedding china."

Laurette makes a sudden noise that is part grinding and part shriek. Rainey waits her out. Finally Laurette says, "I've got no place to store anything."

"You do," says Rainey. "Our townhouse basement." Either the water will dry up, she thinks, or she'll take her Linda-things and that will be the end of it, whichever comes first.

"I don't like it," says Laurette.

"Yes, you do." Rainey combs her fingers through her own long hair as if she were younger, innocent, no possible harm to anyone. "You come over and check on your stuff. Make sure it's safe. And it will be. Safe."

Laurette bites her lip ferociously. "Oh, God," she says. "Oh, God." Her shoulders shake. She propels herself out of the pink chair and paces the narrow aisle. "Why?" she says. "Why would you help me?"

Rainey gathers herself for this moment. She sits up straight and gazes at Laurette. She tries to make her pupils dilate. "I haven't seen Linda in years," she says, bringing her voice down to a stage whisper and thinking, *Trust me.* "You're the closest thing I have to a mother."

Laurette nods as if she expected this. "Francis never visits," she says. "He calls every Sunday. He loves me, but visiting gives him a panic attack." She puts her hand over her breast as if her heart might leap out. Francis is an architect in Berkeley now, and Rainey imagines him in a white apartment with white furniture and nothing on the tabletops. *I am your only niece,* Rainey wants to tell Laurette.

Laurette seems to be thinking something over. "Swear to me," she says finally, "as if you were my daughter, that you won't take a thing or throw anything out."

Outside the window, a pigeon takes off from the concrete sill, and a cat lets loose a hunting cry.

Rainey raises her right hand. "As if I were your daughter," she says.

HER MOTHER SAID, FROM mother to daughter. Taking the ring off her own finger and working it onto Rainey's, tightly, so that Rainey had thought, *Now we will always be connected.*

Her mother said, Don't ever let your father get his hands on this. It's worth a lot.

Her mother said, I'm sure they have a telephone there. She picked her cigarette up off the edge of Rainey's nightstand, inhaled.

Her mother said, Don't let men push you around, baby, not with that body.

Out in the hall her mother said, Howard, I could have stayed. All you had to do was stop smiling at me from the goddamn doorway like I was too stupid to stop packing.

BY FOUR O'CLOCK, RAINEY is late for Tina's and Laurette is on a mission. She wants to store most of what's in her boxes in the townhouse basement. "I'm talking about a tiny room," Rainey says. "Ten boxes and some paintings. Not the *maps*, Laurette. Not the perfume bottles."

Her father is going to kill her. *Bringing home more junk.* Laurette opens one carton after another; they disgorge towels and bead necklaces, hotel stationery and old packages of gauze. Rainey's job is to pack it all up again, tuck the flaps in. Laurette can't think this stuff is going to be saved. Rainey's throat hurts from the dusty, papery air, and her head hurts from yearning. She wants to stumble upon copper-plated baby shoes; she wants to unearth a tendril of snipped-off hair.

From a box of tightly packed manila folders, Laurette pulls a black-and-white photo, a shiny eight-by-ten with one broken-off corner, and studies it long enough that Rainey looks up.

It's a picture of the sisters. The girls stand with dripping cones at the beach; they are perhaps nine or ten. Linda beams at the camera, but Laurette looks anxiously to her left as if a stranger were near.

"My *mother.*" Rainey holds one side of the photo and runs a finger over Linda's windblown hair. "You found my mother."

Laurette tugs at the photo. Rainey hangs on. "Tell me more about her," she says.

"We never got along." Laurette stands with her hand out, waiting. "Linda was prettier. She was always laughing, even when nothing was funny. I would be off somewhere drawing. She got all the boys. There really isn't much to say."

Rainey nods. It sounds like her mother as an adult, too. "She never painted?"

"Just sewed." Laurette reaches for the photograph, which Rainey holds out of reach. "She made her own prom dress."

Laurette hesitates, and in the sentence she doesn't speak Rainey hears, *I didn't go to the prom.*

"She taught me," says Rainey. "I can sew on the bias." She smiles at her aunt. "I got the art from you, I guess." The photo is as much a part of her as fingernails and bone. "I can keep this, can't I, Aunt Laurette?"

"Keep it?" Laurette plucks the picture from Rainey's hand and holds it at arm's length. "Is that why we're opening boxes? So you can take my things?"

"No." Rainey feels the fine print of her face being read.

"You were going to take things from the boxes when you stored them."

Rainey shakes her head. But how could she not take things from the boxes? She feels mute, her throat coated in dust.

"I always knew there'd be a thief. I just didn't think it would be my sister's child. Practically a daughter," says Laurette. "Get out."

Instead, Rainey comes closer. She touches Laurette's face. Laurette takes a sharp breath, as if she might slap Rainey. And Rainey is gloriously prepared to receive it. She *deserves* it. But Laurette does not slap. Her eyes fill, and she says, "Go."

Rainey stifles a tiny laugh in her nose. Of course Laurette won't give her the photo. Rainey picks up the carton that holds the files, the one that yielded the picture.

"Put that box down," says Laurette in Rainey's mother's voice.

"I'm digging you out, Laurette. You and the cats."

Laurette plunges both hands deep in her crinkly hair. "I don't trust you," she says. "You have to leave."

"But I'm like a daughter, remember?" She holds the carton out to Laurette. "Keep looking," she says. "You know there's more."

Laurette holds herself stiffly. Rainey sets the box on the floor at her feet. "I'm not afraid of you," says Laurette.

"Look inside," says Rainey. "You're going to see things you haven't seen in years."

Slowly, still rigid, Laurette gazes down at the box. She stoops and walks her fingers across the tops of the files, extracts, this time, a handwritten letter. "Howard won't like it," she sing-songs. "This storage business."

Rainey looks at the tender curve of Laurette's back. She reaches down and gets into a gentle tugging battle over the letter. "Howard told me to come here. He said you would have what I need," she says. "He wants me to be happy."

She puts a tentative hand between the wings of Laurette's shoulder blades. She imagines her aunt's heart beating fast as a bird's in the cage of her ribs.

"That's it," she says, holding the letter and photograph to her chest as Laurette dips into another file. "You can't throw out a daughter. You know that, right? No one can throw out a *daughter*."

HER MOTHER SAID, LET me show you the backstitch, strongest one there is. It goes one stitch forward, half stitch back. Funny, huh? Live your life that well, baby, I'd say you're doing great.

THANK YOU FOR TRYING

Two nights before they see the suicide girl high over the grand staircase at the Metropolitan Museum of Art, Rainey comes to Leah's for dinner.

Leah compulsively checks the fridge and straightens the rows of flan cups. She straightens the edges of her books. She straightens the plates on the table, perfects a space in the closet for Rainey's coat, and drops into the love seat. Rainey is seventeen minutes late. Eighteen. Nineteen. And then she is there, prowling.

"You *still* live like this?" Rainey says, surveying. "You still have no stuff?"

"Like what?" Leah turns off the oven, where lasagna heats. She hates this oven. It's harvest gold. Certain things are meant to be white, specifically these: sheets, appliances, moldings, towels, toilet paper, stationery, plates—though a gold rim is acceptable on the last two. This from her mother, the decorator.

"I don't know, coffee cups?" Rainey is snooping. "Bills? Catalogs? Ceramic poodles?" It's almost charming, as if she urgently needs to know one riveting detail about Leah, and plans to shake it out of her white-box studio apartment. She grabs Leah's sweater. "Magazines?" She shakes the sleeve, and it's nice, this easy grabbing thing. Leah is suddenly grateful not to have stolen anything from Charles River Labs except a few Erlenmeyer flasks.

"Magazines are in the bookshelves." But Rainey would remember: her *Scientific American*s are in chronological order.

"I give up." Rainey drops her purse on the love seat and walks to the bathroom. Leah listens to the sounds of Rainey's absence. Flush. Running water. Pause for toweling. More silence. Lip gloss? The bathroom door opens.

"Jesus, Levinson. You *fold* it? It's dirty and you *fold* it?"

"I like things neat," says Leah. Is this affection? It feels like something she can bask in.

"In the *hamper*?"

Rainey eats two portions of lasagna and two of flan. "I was starving," she says, finishing her flan, and Leah is pretty sure she means it.

"Let's make it a ritual," she says. "Let's go have steak next week. My treat."

Rainey wears less makeup than she did in school: a little sheen on her eyelids and lips. Vaseline, Leah remembers. A strand of Rainey's hair is caught in the shine on one eyelid, and Leah longs to extract it.

"No, only if I treat." Rainey's posture is perfect. It was that way in eighth grade. "Can Tina come?"

Leah feels the whole operation sinking. "You *can't* treat. You said you're broke." Unable to stand it any longer, she reaches across the table and lifts the strand of hair off Rainey's face. It's very long. It might be a yard long. She almost regrets having to release it.

Rainey tosses her head like a horse dismissing a fly. She says, "I can manage. I've *been* managing." She does not have a credit card. She still sells the occasional quilt. She does not have health insurance or an IRA. Leah learns these things because she *asks*. She asks because she feels compelled.

"You know, I could loan you money," says Leah. "Till you sell some work."

Rainey looks at her directly. "Stop trying to rescue me."

"I'm not." Heat flows into Leah's face. Rescuing Rainey is exactly what she wants to do. She thinks they are close enough that rescue is okay. Is she offering too much, or is her face naked?

"Why don't you commission a tapestry?" says Rainey. "That way I'd sell a piece of art, and you'd have something on the walls. It's not normal not to have anything on your walls."

Leah begins to speak and stops. She doesn't want to commission a piece of art. That would be even-steven, if she is going to be honest with herself. Also, she does not want anything on her walls.

She thinks of her mother, the decorator, who used to sometimes grow thin as a bone. "I feel like a vessel of light," her mother once said, back when she wasn't eating. Leah wants that feeling right now, to be a vessel of light, to draw Rainey in like a moth.

"I can't afford it," she says, "but you ought to give me some slides of your work. My mom might have a client who would order a quilt."

"Tapestry," says Rainey. She pauses. "You really think?"

THE NEXT MORNING THEY meet for breakfast at Eat Here Now, and Rainey is cheerful enough to let Leah pay. She hands Leah a little yellow cardboard box that says KODAK. "These are my only slides. You sure your mother will send them back?"

"She's my *mother*," says Leah.

The box opens like a little drawer. Leah pulls it out and holds the first slide up to the light. It shows a complicated—mosaic, to her mind, or something like a kaleidoscope interior. "That's all photographs, letters, things like that," says Rainey. "And silver thread. The woman who owned those things used to sing. She died last year. It's a memory piece."

This sounds sacred to Leah. "I wish I could see it bigger."

Rainey bites her lip.

"Don't worry," says Leah, "my mom has a slide projector," because this sounds like a promising thing to say. She pulls out a second slide, a close-up of the first. Holding it up to the light, she makes out a watch face and a passport stamp. "These are exquisite," she says, and she is just going for a third slide when Rainey touches her wrist.

"They might get sticky," Rainey says. "I brought tape for the box."

Obediently, Leah returns the slides to the little drawer and watches Rainey fastidiously tape both ends.

"Even one commission, my God," says Rainey. "She'll really show them around?"

"She said she would. She likes unusual things. She likes *the touch of the artist's hand.*"

"You could save my life," says Rainey.

After work Leah goes home and tucks the box of slides into a safe corner of her bookshelves.

Leah has offered money. She's offered meals. Now, just taking the slides in her hand, she feels like a rescuer.

FIRST IMPRESSION LEAH GETS of the suicide girl is white shins and a pair of Candie's platform sandals dangling over the limestone ledge, about twenty-five feet in the air above her.

The second-story ledge encircles the grand staircase at the Metropolitan Museum, and the owner of the shins seems to float up there, suspended over the foot of the stairs. Petite and trembling, the suicide girl plants her hands at her sides as if she intends to propel herself down.

It's 6:00 P.M. A chamber orchestra plays to the lobby crowd, and Leah, on the ground floor beneath the ledge with Rainey and Tina, can't stop staring. Around the girl, the gray fluted columns and balusters and the benchlike ledge she's sitting on seem frigid as architecture carved from ice. She must be freezing, thinks Leah, who is bundled in a raccoon jacket, a cast-off from her mother. She grabs Rainey's arm, ignoring Tina's glance. Rainey gives her a sad little smile and lets Leah keep the arm. It feels good in Leah's hand, resilient and lean.

Rainey wanted to see the jewelry, and she's brought Tina, who lives with her. They are twenty-five, and Leah is still nervous about Tina.

Many people start talking at once. More hands fly to mouths. People stare up at the girl as if she were some bright bird flown in from the zoo.

The girl looks over the people massing below her and on the second floor with a darting, startled gaze. To get to the high ledge, which rims three sides of the stairwell, she must have climbed over a granite railing upstairs; and because she has tucked herself in a corner against a massive pillar, the guards can't sneak up from behind. It's cold in October for her sandals, and her clothes are out of season, too; she wears a summery, finch-green dress.

A guard upstairs begins admonishing the girl. More

people drift to the base of the staircase to see. *Don't push,* snaps Rainey. Her long hair flies with static electricity and seeks the coats of people squeezing past. Tina stands to the side, letting the crowd part around her and looking up at the girl in green as if, Leah thinks, she were a puzzle Tina had to solve. Lilies opiate the air. Men and women in dark, gorgeous clothes spill toward the stairs from the lobby; the air is electrified in that area, and pulses of murmuring grow urgent. Leah, still gripping Rainey's arm, glances at her; she guesses it's not the pushing Rainey minds but the spectacle being made of the girl, who looks ready to cannonball from the second floor.

Near Rainey and Leah, a woman with taut, shiny skin and eager eyes says to her companion, "What's she going to do from up there? Break a fingernail?"

Tina tips her head and says, "Is that your medical risk assessment?"

The woman colors and looks away.

You'll love Tina, Rainey had said. *She's become this totally earnest person.* Leah has a tiny seizure of jealousy over this, because sometimes she wants to bind Rainey to her the way Orthodox men bind phylacteries to their arms.

Leah suspects that Tina, who is even lovelier than in high school, would have something to say about this binding business. Tina has changed. She is a fourth-year medical student. She is a tall, lean column of black with a slash of red lipstick. She looks serene in her beauty now. Her eyes have teaspoons of shadow beneath them. She's almost Dr. Dial. Leah, who had fantasies of being Dr. Levinson, lives only a vaguely scientific life. She swabs the vaginas of sweet-tempered rats to see if, under a microscope, the cells look like cornflakes yet. If they do, that means the rats are in estrus and ready to mate. Leah makes nineteen thousand a year breeding laboratory rats and mice for Charles River in New Jersey.

As the gathering at the foot of the grand staircase packs in and people from the lobby press to see what's going on, the murmur ebbs, then rises. Guards gather in tight blue clusters and try to keep people back. An upstairs guard reaches toward the girl across the balusters. *You have to get off there, Miss. Walk real careful. Take my hand.* But the huge pillar stands between them, and the girl just stares at the floor below.

In the lobby the chamber ensemble plays something sweet and fresh that makes Leah think of rainwater streaming between cobblestones.

People have gathered up and down the stairs as if they were bleachers. "You can't sit there," another guard calls up to the girl, as if this were merely an infraction of the rules. Abruptly Tina shoulders her way toward him. He is young and, Leah is sure of it, shaking. She watches them confer. She peers over the heads of the people packed around her. Leah can see over most people in a crowd, even the women with Farrah Fawcett hair.

She wonders if Rainey will want her arm back soon. Leah is going to need it, if the suicide girl falls. Also, she likes its proximity. A sudden memory hits her of Rainey, in eighth grade, kicking a dodgeball into her face, and Tina laughing, and she flushes with shame.

"She must be crazy to want to die like this," Leah whispers.

"She doesn't want to die," says Rainey.

"Honey," Tina calls up, and her voice is a clear chime. The chatter quiets. "Sweetie. It's never as bad as you think. What can I do? You want to tell me why you're up there?"

The girl smacks one foot hard against the wall, and her sandal sails off. It hits a man on the shoulder when it falls, and a flinch ripples through the crowd. "No." She has a raspy, little-girl voice that should be selling Q-tips, Leah thinks. "I don't want to talk about it."

Very gently, Rainey extracts her arm. Leah wonders if it was simply the arm's time to be released, or if it was the sound of Tina's voice.

Several more guards appear at the foot of the stairs and begin gesturing for the crowd to move. Some people are almost directly beneath the girl, and the guards form a phalanx and usher them back toward the gift shop. Someone shouts, "Is there a doctor?" and from far back in the lobby someone else calls, "Cardiac surgeon, coming through."

"You don't have to talk about it, sweetie." Tina stands in her black turtleneck and jeans, looking and sounding to Leah exactly like what she is, a medical student who rotates through a slum gynecology clinic and has to gain the trust of teenage girls.

"But I think you ought to know," says Tina, "what will happen if you fall."

"DELL," THE BOY SAYS, "I didn't touch her. Please come down."

He's up on the second floor, too, leaning into another pillar and gazing across the top of the staircase at Dell as if this were just one of her stunts. Everyone gets very quiet.

The girl leans over as if the stairwell were a deep pool and she expects to roll forward off the ledge and splash. Which, thinks Leah, in a sense she might. She imagines, crazily, that the girl might spread her wings and take flight over the lobby, green belly flashing above the crowd. "You love her," the girl says, and her voice echoes over the staircase.

"I didn't touch her," the boy calls. Which is not the same, Leah thinks, as *I don't love her.* "For Chrissake, Dell."

"What a prize," says Rainey.

"Get a ladder," calls a guard, which is ridiculous; the girl is maybe twenty-five feet in the air.

Tina cups her hands to her mouth and says loudly, "Honey?" and even the guards look at her. Even the boy looks at her, and Dell sits back up and looks at her. Tina lowers her hands and stands in the center of the floor at the bottom of the grand staircase. "If you fall, can I tell you? You won't die, honey," Tina says. "You'll break a few ribs, maybe crack your skull. If you break the wrong vertebrae you could end up in a wheelchair for the rest of your life. But no way you're gonna die."

"Oh my God," Leah murmurs through her fingers, "she could fall on her *face*."

"I might die if I stand," says the girl. She kicks off the other sandal, causing another mass flinch.

Then she does stand, gingerly, bare toes curled around the edge of the granite.

Two guards climb over the balusters from either side and move stealthily toward her, but she whirls to each side, causing everyone to gasp. "Don't come any closer," she says, and the guards hesitate.

"Honey, come down the long way and talk about it," says Tina. "No guy is worth this kind of damage."

The girl shakes her head.

"She's doing great," Rainey says quietly to Leah, "but they don't train them for this."

Dell shakes her head till her whole upper body begins to sway as she stands on the ledge.

Leah hears the squall of sirens rise to a pitch outside, then cease. A man appears at Tina's side. "I'm a cardiac surgeon," he says. "Who needs me?" He looks around. Then he sees where everyone else is looking, looks back at Tina, and says nothing.

"Dell!" says the boy, and stops. *Don't stop*, thinks Leah.

"That's it?" says the girl. "Just *Dell*? That's all you have to say?"

From the second floor, silence. "Tell her you love her, asshole," someone says loudly.

Rainey whispers, "Someone needs to give that child a script."

Two policemen rush from the front door through a channel that opens in the crowd as the girl in the green dress either slips or loses her nerve for the dive and lets herself fall sideways, flailing, about six feet in front of where Tina stands. Leah hears her land both hard and soft, with a percussive thud.

THAT NIGHT THEY SIT on the museum steps above Fifth Avenue. Rainey and Leah smoke. "I quit in anatomy," says Tina, waving away Leah's offer of a cigarette. "My cadaver's lungs were the color of dog shit."

"Thank you for that detail," says Rainey.

"Just trying to save your life, Rain." *Lives*, thinks Leah, turning her head to blow her smoke away from Tina. *My life, too.* "God, I wanted to save that girl," says Tina.

"You did save her," says Rainey. "She didn't dive."

"She's got broken ribs, a broken ankle, and God knows what internal damage. I wanted to walk her out of there. Away from that *pendejo*."

Leah is afraid to break the moment by asking her exactly what it means. Rainey must know because she doesn't ask.

"She was begging him to come in the ambulance," says Tina. "He didn't want to go, can you imagine?" After a silence, she lowers her face into her hands and says, "I should have gone up on that ledge. I didn't know what I was doing."

"If you'd walked up the stairs to the ledge," says Rainey, "she'd have jumped sooner. You're probably the reason she didn't do a swan dive."

Tina nods into her hands and sniffs. Then she sits up. "The girls at the clinic, they all think their life revolves around some guy. You want to shake them. Just give me one who believes in her own self."

Rainey says, "You don't believe your life revolves around some guy? Come on."

"You think I'm going thirty thousand bucks into debt so I can be some lovesick chick diving over a staircase?" says Tina. "I don't have time for guys. I need sleep. I need six hours of sleep for once in my life."

"I have guys up to my ears," says Rainey. "They don't leave. Remember Jay, with the guitar? Remember the parrot guy? But no one my life should revolve around. Maybe Flynn." She leans forward, chin on her elbows, and looks across Tina at Leah. "What about you, Lee-lee?"

Teen, Rain, and Lee-lee. Leah is ecstatic. It's the first real affection-thing she's heard from Rainey in a while, and she wonders what would be the most casual way to step through this opening door. Certainly she has nothing to report about any guys.

"My life revolves around rats." She laughs. No one else does. "I mean—"

"Wait, I almost forgot," says Tina. Leah stops talking. Tina reaches into her bag and pulls out a white envelope. She hands the envelope to Rainey, who puts it in her own bag.

Money, Leah thinks.

And if that's true, why is Tina allowed to help when she is not? Plus there's something about how Tina does it that takes her breath away. No thanks are needed, and none given. It's so effortless it's almost reckless, like steering with no hands. It makes her jealous all over again.

She clears her throat.

"Hey, I sent your slides out," she says.

It's only been two days. So it's barely a lie. More like an elision of time, since she will still mail the slides. She *will* mail them. "I used Federal Express," she says, unable to stop the story from traveling forward. "So she would have just gotten them." Now it's a lie. But barely. She'll send them tomorrow. She'll use FedEx for real.

"Her mother is a decorator," Rainey tells Tina. "Her clients might buy my work. You know what a big deal that would be?"

"What a sweetheart," says Tina. She means Leah, but she drapes an arm around Rainey for a moment and squeezes her shoulder. Leah looks sidelong at the two of them leaning into each other, Rainey blowing her smoke straight up at the night sky.

"When will she know?" Rainey asks.

"I don't know," says Leah. "A week or two?"

"We should meet back here. We should reclaim this place." Rainey shivers audibly and pulls her denim jacket close. "Or it will always be the suicide museum."

Who is *we?* thinks Leah. Is Tina part of this *we?*

Tina takes off her scarf and wraps it around Rainey's neck. "We'll come back in two Tuesdays and hit the jewelry like Rainey wants. It'll be healing."

"See, that's why I love you," Rainey says.

Why, thinks Leah, why do you love her? She knows why she loves Rainey Royal, who is both cruel and kind, who works with objects that belong to the dead, who can sweep her gaze across Leah's white-box life and make her feel, if only for an hour, that she is the most thrilling person Rainey knows.

AS IT TURNS OUT, Helen Levinson does indeed have a slide projector. She has an assistant who makes prints from all the slides. She sends Leah back the little yellow box, again by FedEx, with a note.

> *Been using black roses and black tulips together—hard to find but stunning. Love this gal's work. Can she compose in all white/cream with many textures? Fabric, paper, buttons, like in slides, but all white. If yes, can commission for two clients now. Have her call me. Love you, darling. My New York rep!*

217

When they meet again at the museum it is even colder. Rainey wears Tina's scarf and gloves.

They sit on the steps with their cigarettes, Tina, again in the middle, in a long down coat, bare hands jammed in her pockets. Leah fingers in her own pocket the yellow cardboard box of slides.

My mother loved your work, she will say. She hopes her voice won't crack.

"My mother loved your work," Leah says, and she pulls out the yellow box and holds it close on her lap.

"Tell me, tell me." Rainey clasps her hands together in Tina's purple gloves.

Tina looks at Leah with bright, expectant eyes. Again Tina and Rainey sit close for warmth, while between Tina and Leah there is a politeness gap of about twelve inches, the gap of two people who have a close friend in common, but not much more.

Rescue is a big deal, Leah thinks.

"Before I forget?" she says. "I wanted to tell you, I'm gone all day. At work. My dining table has nothing on it. Ever. If you wanted to use my place as a studio."

To her amazement this falls into a silence with something hard at the bottom. It reminds Leah of the granite floor at the foot of the grand staircase.

"But she works at home." Tina takes her hands out of her pockets and laces her fingers around her knees, despite the cold. She keeps them still, where Leah's fingers would fidget for a cigarette. Leah thinks: *They've talked about me.*

"Yeah, I know. But if she wanted a studio," says Leah. She tries to keep the edge out of her voice.

"Hello, I'm right here," says Rainey. "I'm fine."

Leah tries to look contrite. "Sorry," she says. "It was a thought." She remembers the envelope Tina passed to Rainey; she wonders if Tina, a medical student, could have given Rainey money or was repaying it—no matter, it was as if they were sharing a tank of air, passing the regulator back and forth.

"Your mother?" prompts Rainey.

My mother loved your work.

Leah takes a breath. "I'm sorry," she says. "She showed prints to her clients. It just didn't happen."

Does Rainey look at her as if she can see Helen's note, read the lines about black roses and white tapestries? It's not possible. And yet Leah could swear that she does.

She waits for Rainey to say, *Thank you for trying. Thank you for trying, Lee-lee.*

After a moment Leah says, "I really tried," exactly as Rainey starts to speak. They both stop, talk at the same moment again. Leah laughs. Rainey waits. Leah lurches on.

"My mother showed them to everyone, but it just—she said she's sorry."

Rainey nods. She holds out her hand, resting her arm on Tina's knees. For a split second Leah thinks she is extending her hand in friendship. Then she understands. She relinquishes the yellow Kodak box.

Leah opens her mouth, but stops. She can't think of a reason to ask for the slides back. The box vanishes into Rainey's purse.

ONE YEAR LATER, ON the day Rainey buries her father, Leah will want to fix this, to seal things between them. Tina will stand as close to Rainey as a bodyguard. Leah will almost do it anyway, will almost say: *We came so close last time—let's send my mom new slides.* But Helen might slip. She might give Leah away. *Where were you two years ago,* Helen might say. *I was waiting for your call.* And then Leah might see ice in Rainey's eyes.

ARRHYTHMIA

Midnight in a house where strangers wander: Rainey's door should be shut tight. But Tina, from the staircase, sees into Rainey's pink room—blush walls, pooling fuchsia curtains. On rough nights, this room reminds Tina of the inside of someone's mouth.

It's every bit her business. She steps inside.

Lying on the canopy bed is a silver-haired man with long, curled toenails and a pregnancy gut. He is reading a battered paperback. A black French-horn case is parked on the floor. He looks comfortable.

Tina says calmly, "I don't think you belong here, motherfucker."

Tina herself has been installed in the hundred-year-old townhouse with Rainey and Howard since her grandmother died. *Gracias a Dios*, she got through medical school rent-free.

Now she's a resident; she's ob-gyn. She works eighty-hour weeks. She can nap standing up. She hallucinates flashes of light, which is happening now, after sixteen hours on her feet.

The silvery man dog-ears his book and swings his legs off the bed. "Apologies, sister," he says. Tina sees he's not as old as he looks, just stringy. "No need to yell," he says.

"Am I yelling?" says Tina. "Who did you think was going to show up?"

Not quite meeting her eyes, he shambles toward the door and edges past her. "Apologies," he says. He limps with his horn up the stairs toward the servants' quarters. Tina's own room is on the fifth floor, too. She has come home from the hospital several times to find one ropy musician or another rooting through her bureau drawers.

"Go down," Tina says, "not up. Go home."

The man looks over the banister at her. "I've played with Dollar Brand," he says. "Don't know who *you* are, but Howard Royal invited me. This is *his* house."

"Not quite," says Tina.

She has never heard of Dollar Brand. And she knows for sure this is no longer Howard's house. She feels Howard's time here is waning. Tina spent half her teenage life in Rainey's pink room; she knew the worshipful young musicians whom Howard took in. She helped pack their shit up last year when Rainey turned twenty-five, took over as trustee, and threw them out while Howard roared.

Now Howard brings home stray musicians one night at a time, and chicks he meets at the clubs. Tina comes down for breakfast, and some sleepy bimbo will be all *Hey, you know where they keep the coffee?* It cuts her every time, but she keeps her feelings to herself. It seems to her that if you play jazz like Howard, you should live in harmony with its godly source. But Howard's godly source seems to vanish when he rises from the piano.

Anyway, he refuses to move out. He lives off Rainey's trust. Rainey can't evict her own father, can she? Rainey can't even put Howard's shadow, Gordy, in the street. Tina regards the listing shadows of the staircase and listens to the ragged footsteps. *Howard, where would you go?*

"You're trespassing," Tina calls, but already she hears the horn player padding toward his room.

WHEN RAINEY GETS HOME from Flynn's she sits on Tina's bed, because her own is polluted: *long toenails.* Now Tina will have to strip Rainey's bed before she sleeps, and probably make it, too. She makes a flawless bed. She can iron the ruffles on a Sunday blouse and cook *rellenos de papas* and mango flan. Her grandmother taught her the domestic arts from her wheelchair.

Rainey says, "You think it'll kill him?"

"It might," says Tina. She closes her eyes and slips into a micro-nod over her unopened beer.

"You're not helping," says Rainey. "I'm not locking him

out forever. I'll let him back in when he calms down. So he can find his own place."

Tina opens her beer and gives Rainey a long, waiting look. Next to her bed is a tiny window to which darkness cleaves. Tina leans over and pulls the string on the roller shade for privacy, and the room becomes a box.

"He won't stay," says Rainey. "Without his own key, he won't stay."

Tina swallows deeply, looking at Rainey over the bottle and saying nothing.

"You think he'll hate me?" Rainey takes the bottle and drinks.

"Howard loves you to death." Tina hesitates. "Does he have enough to move out?"

"He can give lessons," says Rainey. "He can work like a normal person."

"Howard's not a normal person." Tina tugs the bottle from Rainey's hand. "He can't afford the kind of place they let you put a Steinway."

"Jesus, whose side are you on?"

"Yours," says Tina promptly. She watches Rainey: cross-legged at the foot of the bed, carefully separating out a long, thick strand of hair like she intends to make something with it. They haven't braided each other's hair in years. Tina shivers. It's chilly up here in winter. She has one of the dreary little rooms where servants once slept on creaky narrow bedsteads and suffered cracked windows in winter. Her clothes are in a nineteenth-century maple wardrobe, and her medical school textbooks are lined up on a battered desk she dragged in from another room.

Howard has the entire second floor. Sneaking down to see him is not easy. She has to get past Gordy and Rainey, who share the third floor. Tina has been sneaking in to see Howard, one way or another, since she was sixteen.

Now she is twenty-six, and Howard walks with a twinge in his hip, and sometimes when they meet in the shabby rooms of other musicians they lie on the bed fully dressed, and he holds her while she dozes.

"Maybe you should talk to him one more time," says Tina.

To live like this, Tina has closed a door in her head so heavy no light can leak through. She finds she likes living in airtight, watertight compartments.

"I've tried talking. I'll be supporting him and Gordy till they're ninety."

Tina considers this. She herself grew up taking care of her grandmother, while downstairs her mother lived with Tina's sisters, and across the city, her father lived with a woman who worked in a courthouse cafeteria. Someone had to bathe the grandmother, dress her each day in dignified black. But Tina's *abuela* kept her studying at the Formica kitchen table; she kept her sane. She exalted her to *be a doctor* when Tina was busy failing ninth grade. And what were her sisters doing now? They were married, making babies, laboring at stoves with saffron-scented steam.

"My future husband will love it," says Rainey. "He'll really want to stick around."

Tina nods slowly. She has no future husband; she works too hard. Occasionally she's afflicted by a tattoo artist, though he sees other women, and last month, when he took her to City Island, she fell asleep over fried clams. Tina will not let him tattoo so much as a bumblebee on her foot. She is a *doctor.* It isn't funny.

Howard is not husband material, though he teaches her about life. And it is true that Howard drives Rainey's boyfriends away with sarcasm and sexual innuendo, and it is true that Rainey has someone wonderful. She has Flynn, who years ago quit Juilliard for Howard Royal.

Then he quit Howard for medical school. Flynn is an oncologist now, a man who battles cells that simultaneously multiply and divide. Flynn is as delicate and lean as an egret, and his focus is quick and sharp like a bird's, too.

Tina keeps the faith with Rainey in this one department: she ignores Flynn. She remembers how Flynn and Rainey used to stare at each other across the parlor, silent over Howard's jazz. Meanwhile Howard would pin Tina with his gaze from the piano, and Tina's abdominopelvic region would caramelize. It wasn't just the way he made her feel *seen*; it was his hands on the keyboard—those strong, spread, prancing fingers.

"Oh, God. I'm scared." Rainey takes the bottle from Tina and drains the beer. "'How sharper than a serpent's tooth,'" she says. "He always mocks me in Shakespeare."

Tina pulls her folded nightgown out from under her pillow. She needs sleep, but she won't undress in front of Rainey. *When you change*, her grandmother instructed, *don't look down*, and she meant when Tina was alone.

"I'm not trying to save you from hurting Howard," says Tina. She speaks slowly, feeling out which of her words are true and which just sound good. "I'm trying to save you from hurting yourself."

TINA HOLDS RAINEY'S HAIR so she can throw up. She pours Rainey a shot of Jack Daniel's for strength. But she won't dredge up the yellow pages so Rainey can call an all-night locksmith. That Rainey has to do herself.

Howard Royal and Gordy Vine are out, playing an uptown club.

Tina falls onto her bed fully dressed. Screw the nightgown. She leaves Rainey waiting for the locksmith on the stoop, pretending to be a locked-out person and wearing Tina's down coat and fleece-lined boots. Rainey's own clothes are never warm enough. God, she can be such a waif.

Tina wakes when Rainey comes into her room. She hears her lay a brass key on the nightstand and feels her climbing into the twin bed. They have never shared a bed. Don't snuggle, Tina prays. Rainey doesn't snuggle.

"He let me keep the old lock," she whispers. "Guess what it's called."

Tina makes a *don't wake me* noise.

"A cylinder," says Rainey. "Like on a gun."

Tina feels she is falling. She lets herself fall. It's glorious. An insistent ringing wakes her.

Not morning. Please God not morning. She lunges over Rainey for the clock. It's only 4:45. She can sleep till 5:30. Ringing won't stop. *Doorbell.*

"Help me." Rainey sits up. "I'm going to throw up again."

"Not in bed," says Tina. The doorbell is a steady rasping ring.

"Tina, he'll kill me."

"Did you change the basement lock?" Maybe Howard's key will work there.

"Duh."

Tina hears a sound she recognizes in the dark from her rotation in the ER. It's the irregular dental clicking of terrified patients: Rainey's teeth are chattering. It sounds like a Teletype in old movies.

"I need Flynn," says Rainey.

"You could call him," says Tina, "but he needs sleep like I do."

"What if Howard breaks down the door?"

"It's unbreakable." The door is a heavy wrought-iron grille with glass on the inside. Tina thinks of him outside in the frost and wants to be there, wants to put her hand gently on his arm: *Howard, take it easy.*

"You could let him in," says Tina. "He might talk now."

"I'm scared. I want him to call me. There's a pay phone on Sixth."

The bell rings and rings. Along with it, faint and distant, comes a high-pitched metallic banging that could be keys slamming into scrolled ironwork.

Rainey hugs her knees. "Will you go down and talk to him?"

"Fuck no," says Tina. "Wait till he calls."

The doorbell stops ringing.

"If he calls, will you talk to him?"

"He's your father, sweetie." Tina's words slur; she's that tired. "Tell him if he calms down et cetera, you'll let him in."

"I can't," says Rainey. "You tell him."

"Practice," says Tina. "Just say it."

Now the silence is almost as loud as the doorbell.

Rainey draws in a breath, holds it a few seconds, and says, "Did you ever go to bed with my father?"

"Are you seriously asking me that?" says Tina. "Seriously?"

"Well . . ." Rainey ducks her head, and her hair covers her face; she sounds like a little girl. "I just want to say it would be like cheating." Tina stays dramatically silent. "I mean, sometimes I hear you on the stairs late at night." Tina waits. "Creaking," says Rainey. "It freaks me out."

Silence from downstairs.

"And you wait till now to ask me? I get insomnia," says Tina. "I drink some wine. I sit in the parlor. I would rather die than sleep with Howard. Nothing personal."

She listens to Rainey think. She waits for Rainey to say, *Yeah but I never hear the bottom flight creak*, and she understands that Rainey is either filling in the missing creaks or counting them. In the quiet she drifts off for a second or an hour; she isn't sure.

FOUR NIGHTS THAT WEEK Tina awakens to the banging of keys and the doorbell's persistent shrill. It lasts about fifteen minutes, she thinks. She has no idea where Howard sleeps. She misses the smell of his sheets, the velvety irony in his voice. In the mornings Rainey, hollow eyed, says nothing. But the shopping bags she left in the front garden, holding clothes and money for Howard and Gordy, are gone.

On the fifth night's visit the banging barely begins when it stops. After a long moment of silence the telephone rings. Did Howard sprint to Sixth Avenue? Tina stumbles into the hall and answers.

It isn't Howard. It's Gordy. He says he is phoning from the neighbors'.

"I just called an ambulance," says Gordy. "You better come down."

Tina runs downstairs in her pajamas and socks. Rainey calls from her bedroom, "Don't let him in." From blocks away a siren begins its song.

Tina spots only her reflection in the glass of the front door and cups her hand to it, peering out. The bulb in the lantern has been dead for months. No Gordy, no Howard. She pulls open the heavy door, shivers, and scans the empty sidewalk. Darkness is on the block like a lid. Streetlamps are on a short distance away, and snow billows through clouds of light. Tina glances down.

Howard is a dark form on the stoop.

"Oh, baby," she murmurs. Then she turns and calls, "Rainey." Snowflakes whirl into the foyer. Tina shoves Gordy's trumpet case down the stairs and unzips Howard's parka. "Baby, wake up. Wake up for me."

The siren howls distantly from the direction of Saint Vincent's. Howard is no longer an asshole, no longer a teacher, no longer a lover. He is a man Tina has to save. Disobeying every rule she knows, she bolts back inside, losing critical seconds, and shouts, "Rainey!" Then she straddles Howard under the sifting snow, crosses her palms over the face of a black man on his T-shirt, and pumps and pumps. Howard lies inert. He must be kidding. It is one of his sick jokes, like when he slowly felt up one of the girl musicians right in front of her, smiling at Tina the whole time. The man on his shirt has to be a musician. There's lettering under his face, but her arms and the darkness obscure it. She lunges forward, pinches Howard's nose closed, and breathes hard into his mouth, twice.

Strange that they call it the kiss of life. She knows what it means to kiss Howard Royal, whose mouth, he told her, had muscles—a strong mouth. *Embouchure*, he called it. *You feel it, baby?* From the clarinet. But this is nothing like a kiss. This is all business.

She is just pumping again when Gordy comes from next

door with a ridiculous pom-pom hat pulled low over his forehead and says, "Don't stop."

Tina would never stop. "I'm not stopping," she says, panting. A few minutes in, she feels a rib break, a thick icicle. An ambulance wails around the corner and onto their block. Where is Rainey? Why does her own mouth taste of cigarettes? Tina keeps going, but she is sure that Howard has left her, the way he stares up past the cornice with disinterest, and she knows from her grandmother that the dead only come back as ghosts. Tina pumps. She pumps. She remembers that Howard smokes; she remembers the taste of his mouth. Rainey does not materialize. The ambulance sails to a silent stop outside their door, its red eye flaring.

Lights come on in two townhouses across the street.

Two EMT guys gently pull Tina back. The bigger one takes over pumping Howard's heart, and the other takes Howard's carotid pulse for a long time. "You tried," he finally says. "You did good. I saw you. We'll need some information."

SATCHMO. The lettering on the T-shirt says SATCHMO.

Gordy sits on the snowy steps, bent, his forehead resting on Howard's calf.

"Let his daughter say good-bye." Tina runs up to Rainey's bedroom and peels the top of her quilt down. "Rainey," she says, "he can't yell at you." She can't say *dead*. "He isn't mad anymore. You better come down," she says, and Rainey looks at her with the eyes of someone falling off a roof.

From the stoop, in the strobe of red light, Tina watches her. Howard is on a stretcher. Rainey touches his beard.

"I killed him," she says, almost marveling.

Tina sees Rainey, barefoot, on the sidewalk in a delicate frost, and she feels the snow through her own thick socks. She sees Rainey press her cheek to Howard's, and feels the stubble prick her own skin.

WHEN RAINEY CALLS THE clinic the next day, Tina's looking at the plump, puckered cervix of a sixteen-year-old girl. She spins away on her stool and gets the sample IUD and dangles it by its string.

"Look how small," she says.

"No way you're sticking that in me," says the girl.

The high school intern knocks and hands in a green message slip. "The lady said it couldn't wait," she says. "Sorry."

No autopsy, says the slip.

"Just take care of me," the girl says. She wears a silver band around one toe and has neatly painted her toenails white. Her vagina is pretty, a little purse. Tina wonders if male gyns get picky about their lovers' vaginas, or if it all becomes a field of pink and hair. It is something she wishes she could ask Flynn, laughing, intimate, in the way that she wishes she could fuse with all of Rainey's men.

"Let me make an appointment for this, too," Tina says. "You'll barely feel it."

On the message slip, it says, *Thank God*.

"No thanks," says the girl.

"I still have to make a referral," says Tina. "I don't do abortions."

She has never said this before. She can get fired for saying it.

Of course there would be no autopsy; it was just a heart attack. But what if Howard had a congenital arrhythmia? If he did, sudden rage could short-circuit his heart so it quivered instead of pumped.

Tina sees it glossy and shivering, failing its true purpose.

Rainey could have this condition, too. Brugada Syndrome, maybe, or Long Q, one of those.

"You're not paying attention," says the girl. "You're supposed to take care of me."

Tina loves Rainey more than she loves anyone.

"I want to get on with my life," says the girl.

Also, there is this.

Rainey could get tested to see if she has this grenade in her chest. If she does, she could live serenely. Have a placid marriage. Say *om*. Certainly don't go plunging into cold water. Screw the Jersey Shore.

But if she has it, Rainey would know she could die at any time. She might hate Tina Dial for letting her lock Howard out, for being the messenger, something.

Tina's not risking that. Four years ago she lost her grandmother. Rainey Royal she loves so much, she doesn't get why God made them both girls.

She should say nothing. Let it be a regular heart attack.

"I don't want another doctor," says the girl. "I want you."

In her mind's eye Tina sees the fetus radiant and slick inside the girl, a second thrumming heart. It's not *First, do no harm*, Tina thinks. It's *First, define harm*.

HOWARD'S DOORKNOB IS COLD in Tina's hand, and the hall is velvety black. She eases the door open.

His room still smells of him. She moves confidently to the bed in the dark and turns on a lamp.

Socks. Books. Records. T-shirts, inside out. He lived like a teenager, except the posters and album covers on his walls were signed and framed, and his name was on some of the albums. *Piano: Howard Royal.* No one has made his bed—Rainey stopped doing that a few years back. The bed's an antique, with carved pineapples on the four posts, and he told Tina once that pineapples meant hospitality.

The room does not feel hospitable now.

Tina wants something Howard cared about. Something that feels like him in her hand, or triggers her olfactory lobe; or a photo—something Rainey won't miss.

Not his nightstand drawers; she knows what's there. His bureau, maybe. She scans the room in dim light. Between the windows, under stacks of paper that render it almost useless, stands a narrow desk.

Though she's sure it's full of sheet music and reeds and dried-up pens, she tugs gently on the long top drawer. It sticks. She yanks harder. The drawer shrieks. It sounds like a train braking.

Tina freezes. She waits for discovery. For a long moment she stands motionless at the desk and waits. Then she thinks, *What the fuck am I doing? I need to look completely innocent.* Gingerly, she turns her back to the door and starts sifting through papers.

In about a minute the door opens.

"Hi," says Tina. Slowly, she pivots. Her left hand bristles with papers, and she sets them on the desk. Show no weakness, she thinks. Without apology, she says, "I wanted something of his."

"Uh-huh," says Rainey. "I think you left something in his room you didn't want me to find."

Tina stares. This is going to be easier than she thought.

"Oh, please," she says. "I wanted some little memento. Anything. I've known your father since I was a kid, and I barely had a father of my own." Tina silently prays for forgiveness; she has a perfectly good father, he just wasn't around.

"That's all?" Rainey lifts her hair with all ten fingers as if massaging her thoughts. "Why didn't you say?"

"I said it now. I thought it would sound funny if I came out and asked."

Rainey slants a look at her. "It shouldn't sound funny," she says. "Why would it sound funny?"

Suddenly Tina is exhausted. She wants to collapse on the

bed. She also knows that she must not ever, in Rainey's presence, sit on Howard's bed. "I practically grew up here. He was like my second dad," she says, and this time she asks no forgiveness.

Rainey crosses her arms over her red silk bathrobe, stained below the waist. Over the years tiny rips have appeared in the sleeves, and though she sews beautifully, she has not mended them. The bathrobe is an old thing of her mother's, and it touches Tina, the way Rainey can neither give it up nor tend it. "Look me in the eye," says Rainey.

Tina says, "I am looking you in the eye," but it's a lie. She adjusts her gaze.

What does a person need to know about a father? John Dial pages her at work, tells her the facts of his life. *It was just a little blood, baby. A man can cough up a little blood, and it don't mean nothing.* John Dial requires an X-ray, which he refuses to get, and cash, which she does not have. She remembers riding on his shoulders when she was little and now she can't spare a few bucks for the OTB.

The tip of a strand of hair finds its way into Rainey's mouth.

"Okay, here goes," she finally says, and Tina stops breathing. "I'm going to give you something special of his. And it's going to kill me to do it. I want you to know that. Wait here." She leaves the room, her red robe fading into the dark hallway. Tina looks longingly at the bed.

Rainey comes back with her palm extended.

The watch is silver in color, with a worn brown leather band whose cracks are as meaningful and impenetrable to Tina as the creases on Howard's palm. Its face, silvery-white and generous, says HAMILTON. Tina stops herself from mouthing the word. Her heart starts ticking. She had not known until this moment that the watch was what she sought.

She says, surprising herself, "I don't think you should give me that."

"Why not?"

Tina's wrist feels naked already, though she is wearing Paul's watch from ten years back. It dawns on her now that she will have to take Howard's watch off to shower. "Because you'll miss it," she says. *Because I'm going to wear it every second of every day, and you'll always wonder.*

"I know," says Rainey. "I'll miss it the rest of my life."

Tina closes her fingers around the watch and inhales deeply, involuntarily, sighing on the exhale—almost a shudder, as if she had shot up from the bottom of a pool.

She feels Rainey watching her closely.

Rainey says softly, "Teen? I think you should get out of my father's room."

"Absolutely," Tina says.

THE CLARINET HAD KEYS that looked like sterling but weren't and bits of cork inside where the parts met. It didn't seem to Tina there should be cork in a musical instrument any more than there should be Styrofoam in a human body.

"Listen." Howard had been lying on the bed with his head on her thigh, and after she struggled with the fingering for a while—irritated by the tiny vibrations the clarinet sent through her lower teeth—he sat up and took the instrument from her. He played something that was like a scale but short, fewer than eight notes. She thought it might be sharps on the way up, the music climbing a crooked ladder, and then flats on the way down, a kind of sad skidding. Howard could have handed her a tuba, and she would have followed his instructions if it meant sitting on his bed like this, looking at his upside-down face.

"You're bored," he said. "Don't be bored. A scale isn't always major notes. It can be minor, melodic minor, harmonic minor, chromatic—what you just heard."

"I don't know what I heard," said Tina. "I don't have an ear."

"You're right, you don't," said Howard, beaming at her. "If I told you the difference between this"—he put the clarinet to his mouth again and played a note— "and this"—he played virtually the same note—"was of the utmost urgency, would you believe me?"

"I guess," said Tina guardedly. "I don't know. They sound the same."

He set the clarinet between them on his rumpled sheet and took her hand. Her nails were jagged and had peeling pink polish on them, and his were large and clean and shapely. Rainey kept them filed. "If I told you," he said, rubbing her forefinger and then her middle finger, "that the difference between this knucklebone and that knucklebone was of the utmost urgency, would you believe me?"

"Yes," she said. "If you're going to be a doctor, right?"

"It's the same thing," he said. "Notes and knucklebones."

"I'll still never be any good."

"Then be disciplined."

There was weather in his eyes, and in his beard. "I am disciplined," she said. "I'm very disciplined. Can we go to bed now?"

"Ten more times," said Howard. "Show me the fingering ten more times."

He gave her that clarinet, a good one. *A gift should hurt*, he said. She lied and told Rainey it was a loaner. Rainey didn't care what it was—she hurled it into a Dumpster.

Tina told Howard she'd been mugged. "I live in Spanish Harlem," she said, and hated herself for it. Sick with herself, not with him—with the way, after she said *Spanish Harlem*, she let him kiss her again.

She remembers these things the day of Howard's burial. The cemetery is in Queens: damp air clinging to their faces, tamped-down snow crunching underfoot. Today is just family: Flynn, Leah, Gordy, a brother of Howard's and a cluster of older cousins, shivering in dark coats after the minister leaves. Tina pretends she is just at the interment of her best friend's father. *None of this is for me.*

The big jazz funeral, the real thing, is in three weeks

at Saint John the Divine's. Tina can't take off twice. It's killing her.

In her pocket she has a prayer card—one of her grandmother's—to drop into Howard's grave.

Rainey wears a vintage hat with a half veil across her face, and a thrift-store Victorian black blouse that Tina buttoned up the back for her that morning. She wears a floor-length black moiré skirt, another thrift-store find, that trails below her peacoat in the snow. Her hands are bare. "Here, babe," says Tina. She takes off her own purple gloves.

"You look like an Edith Wharton novel," says Leah, touching the high lacy collar of the blouse.

"I wasn't in English that day." Rainey leans into Flynn.

Tina watches Gordy look down at the head of the casket like a man who might jump in. The casket is black, so shiny she could almost lick it. She watches the relatives glancing toward their cars. She fingers the bent edge of her Saint Anthony card, and her head floats, as if the lining of her brain has been suctioned out. She is losing Howard to the ground, and she might be losing Rainey to Flynn. She doesn't know what comfort to offer that Flynn isn't already providing, his arm drawing Rainey in close.

"Why won't you admit that I killed him?" Rainey says in a low voice.

Leah's hand flutters to her mouth. Flynn pulls Rainey in tighter. Tina doesn't flicker. She says, "Because you didn't." She has been telling this half-truth all week. She reaches out and recalibrates Rainey's veil. "Because he had a bad heart; because it was going to happen anyway." She may never get to the next part—Listen, you ought to get tested. Something could set you off, too.

Leah peels her hand off her mouth, staring. After a moment she walks to the mound of dirt, pulls back the tarp, and turns to them holding a shovel. How did she know it was there, Tina thinks, and then, she's going to bury him herself. Leah says, "Rainey?"

"You've lost it," says Tina. "Put that away."

"Sweetie?" says Rainey, peering at the shovel.

"I want—" says Leah. She seems to get stuck there. Everyone is looking at her now, this red-haired girl standing in a cemetery like she plans to move that whole pile of dirt wearing cute boots and a corduroy mini-skirt. Gordy's now inches from the edge of the grave. "I want—"

Tina's tempted to wrestle her for the shovel.

"I want to buy a tapestry." It comes out as one polysyllabic word. "Remember? You said my walls were too bare? I want one now."

Gravestones rise in every direction away from them regular as the Green Stamps Tina's grandmother used to paste into those books. Not far off a stone angel guards a crypt, and his plumage curves and dips in their direction.

"A tapestry," says Rainey. She nods at the shovel. "What about *that*?"

Leah looks down at what she's holding. "Right." Tina sees her trembling, or shuddering, she isn't sure which. "At a Jewish funeral, you'd take one shovel of dirt and . . ." She lifts her chin toward the grave. "For closure," she says.

Rainey wraps her arms around herself. "That sounds unbearable."

But Tina likes it. She thinks of her grandmother's funeral, of Rainey hesitating and then bending to kiss the granite forehead.

"I think it sounds like you," says Flynn. Tina stares at his gloved hand on Rainey's shoulder and feels the pressure through her own coat. And it's not just Flynn, she realizes. It's every man who belongs to Rainey. She will always feel their hands on her.

"I can't drop earth on my father," says Rainey. Which surprises Tina. Because it does sound like Rainey to do the hard thing. *The heart thing.*

"I'll go first," says Tina. *He was mine, too.*

Rainey sniffs hard. "The hell you will," she says. She takes the shovel from Leah, plunges it into the pile of dirt, and fights it out again. Standing above the grave, she shakes off Flynn's protective hand and weaves slightly. She can't seem to release the earth.

"I don't think you're allowed to do that," says one of the Howard cousins, eyeing the shovel. She has a narrow chin with a kerchief tied under it, which satisfies Tina immensely.

"It's our grave." Tina bends back a corner of the card in

her pocket. Saint Anthony, patron saint of lost things, of lost clarinets. Tina's head keeps floating as she works a fingernail along the edge of the prayer card. She wants to send something of herself into the grave. Howard took her teenage years, but he gave her so much. Do your scales, Howard had said. Music will teach you how to live. *Zelosamente*, zealously. *Appassionato*—she knew that one. *Acceso*, on fire.

Howard was an adult. That made it wrong. Tina knows that now. But things were different in the early seventies. Howard was menacingly cool. Tina could get high with him in his room, and he would unbutton her top so slowly that the floor tipped on its axis, and what they were doing would be almost normal, and soon it *was* normal.

Tina telegraphs to Rainey mentally. *I am standing beside you. Heart with you.* Rainey flashes her a look, tilts the shovel, and drops the earth into the grave. Hitting the casket, it rumbles. A sheen breaks out on Rainey's forehead. She looks stricken, Tina thinks.

Tina closes her hands around the shovel. She's not being solicitous. She wants a turn. Rainey pulls it away. She teeters to the mound of earth on her high heels, fills the blade, turns back, and drops more earth into the grave.

Intervals, Howard had called them: distances between the notes. Some intervals, he said, are so small the human ear cannot detect them. What is the interval, Tina wants to know, between staying silent and telling the truth?

"Rain," says Tina, as Rainey goes back for thirds, like she

has a hunger for it. Rainey ignores her and fills the shovel a fourth time, a fifth, making a fight of it. She breaks into a sweat. Her eyes fill. This might be bad for you, Tina thinks, exertion and despair. What is her obligation? She wants to protect Rainey, and she wants to let Rainey bury her father, and she wants her own turn at the grave. She wants to tell Rainey: Take it easy, babe—you might have your father's heart. Howard's beautiful, crazy, fucked-up heart.

In a slow-motion vision that comes to her, Rainey stops stabbing at the earth, turns, culls the long, stray strands of hair from her face and says, looking straight at Tina: *I know everything I need to know about my heart.*

The vision ends. Rainey hands Flynn her peacoat. Again and again she goes back to the dirt, and Tina shadows her, partly to offer some bodily comfort, partly to find the right moment to drop in her card so that Rainey will not spot it. Pebbles and clumps hit the casket like a drumbeat of rain. There's rhythm, almost.

More like arrhythmia.

Words reverberating in her head: *I need to know about my heart.*

Tina palms the Saint Anthony card, readies it against her coat. "Gentlest of saints," the prayer calls him. There was nothing gentle about Howard. Still. It's the right card, and she is ready to let it drop.

She has every right.

Yet it is true that if Rainey sees it fluttering from her hand, or glinting in the grave, it will be as if Tina stepped back into Howard's room.

Tina follows Rainey as she circles the grave, laboring, creating an even tapestry of soil that slowly drapes the casket. She ignores Leah, who paces, watching. She ignores Gordy, standing apart as if he were an island with his grief; at home, his room is full of half-packed boxes. She hears distantly the cousins calling their farewells. After a while, the gleam of the casket is no longer visible.

Listen to every part of the music, Howard had said. Jazz has an inner voice, a melodic line between the melody and the bass.

First, define harm.

Tina slips the Saint Anthony card back in her pocket. Howard's watch is warm against her wrist.

She remembers Rainey saying in a moment of crisis, *I'm great—I have every single thing that I need.* And she wonders what, if anything, she will tell her closest friend.

ACKNOWLEDGMENTS

My gratitude to the National Endowment for the Arts for the Fellowship that supported this work.

To Joy Harris and Rob Spillman: guardian angels.

To Jim Krusoe, for reading first. To Dean Baquet, for reading last. To Tara Ison and Claire Whitcomb for reading with rare generosity and skill. To Natalie Baszile, Michelle Brafman, Susan Coll, Pia Ehrhardt, David Groff, Anne Horowitz, Mary Otis and Janice Shapiro: extraordinary, gifted readers.

To Heather Sellers, who read multiple drafts of everything with love and wisdom. "Arrhythmia" is dedicated to her.

To everyone at Soho Press, in particular Bronwen Hruska, Meredith Barnes, Rudy Martinez, Janine Agro, and the surgically brilliant Mark Doten. I'm so grateful to have landed here. And to Judith Freeman, for the introduction.

To Lisa Lenz. To Lisa Skolnik. To Jenny Krusoe. To Jonathan Weaver, M.D., for literary medical advice (any errors are mine). To Laurent Besson, and Adam Reed.

To my son, Ari Baquet. To my mother, Erica Landis.

Finally I am honored to acknowledge these artists: the late Jeffrey Cook of New Orleans, whose sculpture inspired Rainey's shoe-and-bible sculpture in "I Know What Makes You Come Alive;" Duke Riley of New York, whose work inspired the tattoos of historic New York in "Trash;" and Stephanie Kerley Schwartz of Los Angeles, whose paper quilts and use of metal scraps inspired Rainey's tapestries.